MARGARET

was born in Ottawa in 1939. She spent much of her early life in the northern Ontario and Quebec bush country. A graduate from the University of Toronto, where she won a Woodrow Wilson Fellowship, with a Masters degree from Radcliffe College, she has travelled extensively and held a wide variety of jobs.

Virago publish all Margaret Atwood's works of fiction including her most recent novel, the bestselling *The Robber Bride*, as well as three selections of her poetry, *Morning in the Burned House* (1995), *Poems: 1965–1975* and *Poems: 1976–1986* and a collection of interviews, *Margaret Atwood: Conversations*.

Margaret Atwood lives in Toronto with the writer Graeme Gibson and their daughter.

BOOKS BY MARGARET ATWOOD

FICTION
The Edible Woman
Surfacing
Lady Oracle
Life Before Man
Bodily Harm
The Handmaid's Tale
Cat's Eye
The Robber Bride

SHORT FICTION
Dancing Girls
Bluebeard's Egg
Wilderness Tips
Good Bones
Murder in the Dark

NONFICTION
Survival: A Thematic Guide to Canadian Literature
Second Words

POETRY
The Circle Game
The Animals in That Country
The Journals of Susanna Moodie
Procedures for Underground
Power Politics
You Are Happy
Two-Headed Poems
True Stories
Interlunar
Selected Poems
Selected Poems II
Morning in the Burned House

BONES
AND
MURDER

MARGARET
ATWOOD

Published by VIRAGO PRESS Limited 1995
20 Vauxhall Bridge Road, London SW1V 2SA

First published by Nan A. Talese, an imprint of Doubleday,
a division of Bantam Doubleday Dell Publishing, New York 1994

'Murder in the Dark,' 'Women's Novels,' 'The Boys' Own Annual,
1911,' 'Simmering,' 'Happy Endings,' 'The Victory Burlesk,'
'She,' 'Liking Men,' 'Iconography,' 'Bread,' and 'The Page'
were first collected in *Murder in the Dark* (Toronto: Coach House Press,
1983; London: Virago 1994). All the others, with the exception of
'Simple Murders,' were first collected in *Good Bones* (Toronto: Coach
House Press, 1992; London: Virago 1994).

Some of these pieces have appeared in America and Canada in *Adam*,
Antaeus, *Bread & Roses*, *Exile*, *Fireweed*, *From Ink Lake*, *Island*, *Littfass*,
Liturataz, *The Lunatic Gazette*, *Harper's*, *The Mississippi Review*, *Quest*,
Tamarack Review, *This Magazine*, *Time Out*, and *Toronto Life*; some have
been broadcast on the CBC program *Anthology*.

A CIP catalogue for this book is available from the British Library

Typeset by Keystroke, Jacaranda Lodge, Wolverhampton
Printed in Britain by Cox & Wyman Ltd,
Reading, Berkshire

CONTENTS

CONTENTS

BONES AND MURDER

MURDER
IN THE
DARK

This is a game I've played only twice. The first time I was in grade five, I played it in a cellar, the cellar of a large house belonging to the parents of a girl called Louise. There was a pool table in the cellar but none of us knew anything about pool. There was also a player piano. After a while we got tired of running the punchcard rolls through the player piano and watching the keys go up and down by them-selves, like something in a late movie just before you see the dead person. I was in love with a boy called Bill, who was in love with Louise. The other boy, whose name I can't remember, was in love with me. Nobody knew who Louise was in love with.

So we turned out the lights in the cellar and played *Murder in the Dark*, which gave the boys the pleasure of being able to put their hands around the girls' necks and gave the girls the pleasure of screaming. The excitement was almost more than we could bear, but luckily Louise's parents came home and asked us what we thought we were up to.

The second time I played it was with adults; it was not as much fun, though more intellectually complex.

I heard that this game was once played at a summer cottage by six normal people and a poet, and the poet really tried to kill someone. He was hindered only by the intervention of a dog, which could not tell fantasy from reality. The thing about this game is that you have to know when to stop.

Here is how you play:

You fold up some pieces of paper and put them into a hat, a bowl, or the center of the table. Everyone chooses a piece. The one who gets the *x* is the detective, the one who gets the black spot is the killer. The detective leaves the room, turning off the lights. Everyone gropes around in the dark until the murderer picks a victim. He can either whisper, 'You're dead,' or he can slip his hands around a throat and give a playful but decisive squeeze. The victim screams and falls down. Everyone must now stop moving around except the murderer, who of course will not want to be found near the body. The detective counts to ten, turns on the lights, and enters the room. He may now question anyone but the victim, who is not allowed to answer, being dead. Everyone but the murderer must tell the truth. The murderer must lie.

If you like, you can play games with this game. You can say: the murderer is the writer, the detective is the reader, the victim is the book. Or perhaps, the murderer is the writer, the detective is the critic, and the victim is the reader. In that case the book would be the total *mise en scène*, including the lamp that was accidentally tipped over and broken. But really it's more fun just to play the game.

In any case, that's me in the dark. I have designs on you, I'm plotting my sinister crime, my hands are reaching for your neck or perhaps, by mistake, your thigh. You can hear my footsteps approaching, I wear boots and carry a knife, or maybe it's a pearl-handled revolver, in any case I wear boots with very soft soles, you can see the cinematic glow of my cigarette, waxing and waning in the fog of the room, the street, the room, even though I don't smoke. Just remember this, when the scream at last has ended and you've turned on the lights: by the rules of the game, I must always lie.

Now: do you believe me?

BAD
NEWS

The red geraniums fluorescing on the terrace, the wind swaying the daisies, the baby's milk-fed eyes focusing for the first time on a double row of beloved teeth — what is there to report? Bloodlessness puts her to sleep. She perches on a rooftop, her brass wings folded, her head with its coiffure of literate serpents tucked beneath the left one, snoozing like a noon pigeon. There's nothing to do but her toenails. The sun oozes across the sky, the breezes undulate over her skin like warm silk stockings, her heart beats with the systole and diastole of waves on the breakwater, boredom creeps over her like vines.

She knows what she wants: an event, by which she means a slip of the knife, a dropped wineglass or bomb, something broken. A little acid, a little gossip, a little hi-tech megadeath: a sharp thing that will wake her up. Run a tank over the geraniums, turn the wind up to hurricane so the daisies' heads tear off and hurtle through the air like bullets, drop the baby from the balcony and watch the mother swan-dive after him, with her snarled Ophelia hair and addled screams.

The melon-burst, the tomato-colored splatter – now that's a story! She's awake now, she sniffs the air, her wings are spread for flight. She's hungry, she's on the track, she's howling like a siren, and she's got your full attention.

No news is good news, everyone knows that. You know it, too, and you like it that way. When you're feeling bad she scratches at your window, and you let her in. *Better them than you*, she whispers in your ear. You settle back in your chair, folding the rustling paper.

UNPOPULAR
GALS

1.

Everyone gets a turn, and now it's mine. Or so they used to tell us in kindergarten. It's not really true. Some get more turns than others, and I've never had a turn, not one! I hardly know how to say *I, or mine*; I've been *she, her, that one*, for so long.

I haven't even been given a name; I was always just the ugly sister; put the stress on *ugly*. The one the other mothers looked at, then looked away from and shook their heads gently. Their voices lowered or ceased altogether when I came into the room, in my pretty dresses, my face leaden and scowling. They tried to think of something to say that would redeem the situation – *Well, she's certainly strong* – but they knew it was useless. So did I.

You think I didn't hate their pity, their forced kindness? And knowing that no matter what I did, how virtuous I was, or hardworking, I would never be beautiful. Not like her, the one who merely had to sit there to be adored. You wonder why I stabbed the blue eyes of my dolls with pins and pulled their hair out until they were bald? Life isn't fair. Why should I be?

As for the prince, you think I didn't love him? I loved him more than she did; I loved him more than anything. Enough to cut off my foot. Enough to murder. Of course I disguised myself in heavy veils, to take her place at the altar. Of course I threw her out the window and pulled the sheets up over my head and pretended to be her. Who wouldn't, in my position.

But all my love ever came to was a bad end. Red-hot shoes, barrels studded with nails. That's what it feels like, unrequited love.

She had a baby, too. I was never allowed.

Everything you've ever wanted, I wanted also.

2.

A libel action, that's what I'm thinking. Put an end to this nonsense. Just because I'm old and live alone and can't see very well, they accuse me of all sorts of things. Cooking and eating children, well, can you imagine? What a fantasy, and even if I did eat just a few, whose fault was it? Those children were left in the forest by their parents, who fully intended them to die. Waste not, want not has always been my motto.

Anyway, the way I see it, they were an offering. I used to be given grown-ups, men and women both, stuffed full of seasonal goodies and handed over to me at seed-time and harvest. The symbolism was a little crude perhaps, and the events themselves were – some might say – lacking in taste, but folks' hearts were in the right place. In return, I made things germinate and grow and swell and ripen.

Then I got hidden away, stuck into the attic, shrunken and parched and covered up in fusty draperies. Hell, I used to have breasts! Not just two of them. Lots. Ever wonder why a third tit was the crucial test, once, for women like me?

Or why I'm so often shown with a garden? A wonderful garden, in which mouth-watering things grow. Mulberries. Magic cabbages. Rapunzel, whatever that is. And all those pregnant women trying to clamber over the wall, by the light of the moon, to munch up my fecundity, without giving anything in return. Theft, you'd call it, if you were at all openminded.

That was never the rule in the old days. Life was a gift then, not something to be stolen. It was my gift. By earth and sea I bestowed it, and the people gave me thanks.

3.

It's true, there are never any evil stepfathers. Only a bunch of lily-livered widowers, who let me get away with murder vis-à-vis their daughters. Where are they when I'm making those girls drudge in the kitchen, or sending them out into the blizzard in their paper dresses? Working late at the office. Passing the buck. Men! But if you think they knew nothing about it, you're crazy.

The thing about those good daughters is, they're so *good*. Obedient and passive. Sniveling, I might add. No get-up-and-go. What would become of them if it weren't for me? Nothing, that's what. All they'd ever do is the housework, which seems to feature largely in these stories. They'd marry some peasant, have seventeen kids, and get 'A Dutiful Wife' engraved on their tombstones, if any. Big deal.

I stir things up, I get things moving. 'Go play in the traffic,' I say to them. 'Put on this paper dress and look for strawberries in the snow.' It's perverse, but it works. All they have to do is smile and say hello and do a little more housework, for some gnomes or nice ladies or whatever, and bingo, they get the king's son and the palace, and no more dishpan hands.

Whereas all I get is the blame.

God knows all about it. No Devil, no Fall, no Redemption. Grade two arithmetic.

You can wipe your feet on me, twist my motives around all you like, you can dump millstones on my head and drown me in the river, but you can't get me out of the story. I'm the plot, babe, and don't ever forget it.

THE
LITTLE
RED HEN
TELLS ALL

Everyone wants in on it. Everyone! Not just the cat, the pig and the dog. The horse too, the cow, the rhinoceros, the orangutang, the horned toad, the wombat, the duck-billed platypus, you name it. There's no peace any more and all because of that goddamn loaf of bread.

It's not easy, being a hen.

You know my story. Probably you had it told to you as a shining example of how you yourself ought to behave. Sobriety and elbow grease. Do it yourself.

Then invest your capital. Then collect. I'm supposed to be an illustration of *that?* Don't make me laugh.

I found the grain of wheat, true. So what? There are lots of grains of wheat lying around. Keep your eyes to the grindstone and you could find a grain of wheat, too. I saw one and picked it up. Nothing wrong with that. Finders keepers. A grain of wheat saved is a grain of wheat earned. Opportunity is bald behind.

Who will help me plant this grain of wheat? I said. *Who? Who?* I felt like a goddamn owl.

Not me, not me, they replied. *Then I'll do it myself,* I said, as the nun quipped to the vibrator. Nobody was listening, of course. They'd all gone to the beach.

Don't think it didn't hurt, all that rejection. Brooding in my nest of straw, I cried little red hen tears. Tears of chicken blood. You know what that looks like, you've eaten enough of it. Makes good gravy.

So, what were my options? I could have eaten that grain of wheat right away. Done myself a nutritional favor. But instead I planted it. Watered it. Stood guard over it night and day with my little feathered body.

So it grew. Why not? So it made more grains of

wheat. So I planted those. So I watered those. So I ground them into flour. So I finally got enough for a loaf of bread. So I baked it. You've seen the pictures, me in my little red hen apron, holding the loaf with its plume of aroma in between the tips of my wings, smiling away. I smile in all the pictures, as much as you can smile, with a beak. Whenever they said *Not me*, I smiled. I never lost my temper.

Who will help me eat this loaf of bread? I said. *I will*, said the cat, the dog and the pig. *I will*, said the antelope. *I will*, said the yak. *I will*, said the five-lined skink. *I will*, said the pubic louse. They meant it, too. They held out their paws, hooves, tongues, claws, mandibles, prehensile tails. They drooled at me with their eyes. They whined. They shoved petitions through my mail slot. They became depressed. They accused me of selfishness. They developed symptoms. They threatened suicide. They said it was my fault, for having a loaf of bread when they had none. Every single one of them, it seemed, needed that goddamn loaf of bread more than I did.

You can bake more, they said.

So then what? I know what the story says, what I'm supposed to have said: *I'll eat it myself so kiss off.* Don't believe a word of it. As I've pointed out, I'm a hen, not a rooster.

Here, I said. *I apologize for having the idea in the first place. I apologize for luck. I apologize for self-denial. I apologize for being a good cook. I apologize for that crack about nuns. I apologize for that crack about roosters. I apologize for smiling, in my smug hen apron, with my smug hen beak. I apologize for being a hen.*

Have some more.

Have mine.

GERTRUDE
TALKS
BACK

I always thought it was a mistake, calling you Hamlet.
I mean, what kind of a name is that for a young boy?
It was your father's idea. Nothing would do but that
you had to be called after him. Selfish. The other kids
at school used to tease the life out of you. The nick-
names! And those terrible jokes about pork.

I wanted to call you George.

I am *not* wringing my hands. I'm drying my nails.

Darling, please stop fidgeting with my mirror.
That'll be the third one you've broken.

Yes, I've seen those pictures, thank you very much.

I *know* your father was handsomer than Claudius. High brow, aquiline nose and so on, looked great in uniform. But handsome isn't everything, especially in a man, and far be it from me to speak ill of the dead, but I think it's about time I pointed out to you that your dad just wasn't a whole lot of fun. Noble, sure, I grant you. But Claudius, well, he likes a drink now and then. He appreciates a decent meal. He enjoys a laugh, know what I mean? You don't always have to be tiptoeing around because of some holier-than-thou principle or something.

By the way, darling, I wish you wouldn't call your stepdad *the bloat king*. He does have a slight weight problem, and it hurts his feelings.

The rank sweat of a *what?* My bed is certainly not *enseamed*, whatever that might be! A nasty sty, indeed! Not that it's any of your business, but I change those sheets twice a week, which is more than you do, judging from that student slum pigpen in Wittenberg. I'll certainly never visit you *there* again without prior warning! I see that laundry of yours when you bring it home, and not often enough either, by a long shot! Only when you run out of black socks.

And let me tell you, everyone sweats at a time like that, as you'd find out very soon if you ever gave it a try. A real girlfriend would do you a heap of good. Not like that pasty-faced what's-her-name, all trussed up like a prize turkey in those touch-me-not corsets of hers. If you ask me, there's something off about that girl. Borderline. Any little shock could push her right over the edge.

Go get yourself someone more down-to-earth. Have a nice roll in the hay. Then you can talk to me about nasty sties.

No, darling, I am not *mad* at you. But I must say you're an awful prig sometimes. Just like your Dad. *The Flesh*, he'd say. You'd think it was dog dirt. You can excuse that in a young person, they are always so intolerant, but in someone his age it was getting, well, very hard to live with, and that's the under-statement of the year.

Some days I think it would have been better for both of us if you hadn't been an only child. But you realize who you have to thank for *that*. You have no idea what I used to put up with. And every time I felt like a little, you know, just to warm up my aging bones, it was like I'd suggested murder.

Oh! You think *what?* You think Claudius murdered your Dad? Well, no wonder you've been so rude to him at the dinner table!

If I'd known *that*, I could have put you straight in no time flat.

It wasn't Claudius, darling.

It was me.

THERE
WAS
ONCE

— There was once a poor girl, as beautiful as she was good, who lived with her wicked stepmother in a house in the forest.

— Forest? *Forest* is passé, I mean, I've had it with all this wilderness stuff. It's not a right image of our society, today. Let's have some *urban* for a change.

— There was once a poor girl, as beautiful as she was good, who lived with her wicked stepmother in a house in the suburbs.

— That's better. But I have to seriously query this word *poor*.

— But she *was* poor!

— Poor is relative. She lived in a house, didn't she?

— Yes.

— Then socioeconomically speaking, she was not poor.

— But none of the money was *hers!* The whole point of the story is that the wicked stepmother makes her wear old clothes and sleep in the fireplace —

— Aha! They had *fireplace!* With *poor*, let me tell you, there's no fireplace. Come down to the park, come to the subway stations after dark, come down to where they sleep in cardboard boxes, and I'll show you *poor*!

— There was once a middle-class girl, as beautiful as she was good —

— Stop right there. I think we can cut the *beautiful*, don't you? Women these days have to deal with too many intimidating physical role models as it is, what with those bimbos in the ads. Can't you make her, well, more average?

- There was once a girl who was a little overweight and whose front teeth stuck out, who –

- I don't think it's nice to make fun of people's appearances. Plus, you're encouraging anorexia.

- I wasn't making fun! I was just describing –

- Skip the description. Description oppresses. But you can say what color she was.

- What color?

- You know. Black, white, red, brown, yellow. Those are the choices. And I'm telling you right now, I've had enough of white. Dominant culture this, dominant culture that –

- I don't know what color.

- Well, it would probably be *your* color, wouldn't it?

- But this isn't *about* me! It's about this girl –

- Everything is about you.

- Sounds to me like you don't want to hear this story at all.

- Oh well, go on. You could make her ethnic. That might help.

— There was once a girl of indeterminate descent, as average-looking as she was good, who lived with her wicked —

— Another thing. *Good* and *wicked*. Don't you think you should transcend those puritanical judgmental moralistic epithets? I mean, so much of that is conditioning, isn't it?

— There was once a girl, as average-looking as she was well-adjusted, who lived with her stepmother, who was not a very open and loving person because she herself had been abused in childhood.

— Better. But I am so *tired* of negative female images! And stepmothers — they always get it in the neck! Change it to *stepfather*, why don't you? That would make more sense anyway, considering the bad behavior you're about to describe. And throw in some whips and chains. We all know what those twisted, repressed, middle-aged men are like —

— *Hey, just a minute!* I'm *a middle-aged* —

— Stuff it, Mister Nosy Parker. Nobody asked you to stick in your oar, or whatever you want to call that thing. This is between the two of us. Go on.

— There was once a girl —

— How old was she?

— I don't know. She was young.

— This ends with a marriage, right?

— Well, not to blow the plot, but — yes.

— Then you can scratch the condescending pater-
nalistic terminology. It's *woman*, pal. *Woman*.

— There was once —

— What's this *was, once?* Enough of the dead past.
Tell me about *now*.

— There —

— So?

— So, what?

— So, why not *here?*

WOMEN'S
NOVELS

For Lenore

1. Men's novels are about men. Women's novels are about men too but from a different point of view. You can have a men's novel with no women in it except possibly the landlady or the horse, but you can't have a women's novel with no men in it. Sometimes men put women in men's novels but they leave out some of the parts: the heads, for instance, or the hands. Women's novels leave out parts of the men as well. Sometimes it's the stretch

between the belly button and the knees, sometimes it's the sense of humor. It's hard to have a sense of humor in a cloak, in a high wind, on a moor.

Women do not usually write novels of the type favored by men but men are known to write novels of the type favored by women. Some people find this odd.

2. I like to read novels in which the heroine has a costume rustling discreetly over her breasts, or discreet breasts rustling under her costume; in any case there must be a costume, some breasts, some rustling, and, over all, discretion. Discretion over all, like a fog, a miasma through which the outlines of things appear only vaguely. A glimpse of pink through the gloom, the sound of breathing, satin slithering to the floor, revealing what? Never mind, I say. Never never mind.

3. Men favor heroes who are tough and hard: tough with men, hard with women. Sometimes the hero goes soft on a woman but this is always a mistake. Women do not favor heroines who are tough and hard. Instead they have to be tough

and soft. This leads to linguistic difficulties. Last time we looked, monosyllables were male, still dominant but sinking fast, wrapped in the octopoid arms of labial polysyllables, whispering to them with arachnoid grace: *darling darling*.

4. Men's novels are about how to get power. Killing and so on, or winning and so on. So are women's novels, though the method is different. In men's novels, getting the woman or women goes along with getting the power. It's a perk, not a means. In women's novels you get the power by getting the man. The man is the power. But sex won't do, he has to love you. What do you think all that kneeling's about, down among the crinolines, on the Persian carpet? Or at least say it. When all else is lacking, verbalization can be enough. *Love.* There, you can stand up now, it didn't kill you. Did it?

5. I no longer want to read about anything sad. Anything violent, anything disturbing, anything like that. No funerals at the end, though there can be some in the middle. If there must be deaths, let there be resurrections, or at least a Heaven so we

know where we are. Depression and squalor are for those under twenty-five, they can take it, they even like it, they still have enough time left. But real life is bad for you, hold it in your hand long enough and you'll get pimples and become feebleminded. You'll go blind.

I want happiness, guaranteed, joy all round, covers with nurses on them or brides, intelligent girls but not too intelligent, with regular teeth and pluck and both breasts the same size and no excess facial hair, someone you can depend on to know where the bandages are and to turn the hero, that potential rake and killer, into a well-groomed country gentleman with clean finger-nails and the right vocabulary. *Always*, he has to say, *Forever*. I no longer want to read books that don't end with the word *forever*. I want to be stroked between the eyes, one way only.

6. Some people think a woman's novel is anything without politics in it. Some think it's anything about relationships. Some think it's anything with a lot of operations in it, medical ones I mean. Some think it's anything that doesn't give you a broad panoramic view of our exciting times. Me,

well, I just want something you can leave on the coffee table and not be too worried if the kids get into it. You think that's not a real consideration? You're wrong.

7. *She had the startled eyes of a wild bird.* This is the kind of sentence I go mad for. I would like to be able to write such sentences, without embarrassment. I would like to be able to read them without embarrassment. If I could only do these two simple things, I feel, I would be able to pass my allotted time on this earth like a pearl wrapped in velvet.

She had the startled eyes of a wild bird. Ah, but which one? A screech owl, perhaps, or a cuckoo? It does make a difference. We do not need more literalists of the imagination. They cannot read *a body like a gazelle's* without thinking of intestinal parasites, zoos, and smells.

She had a feral gaze like that of an untamed animal, I read. Reluctantly I put down the book, thumb still inserted at the exciting moment. He's about to crush her in his arms, pressing his hot, devouring, hard, demanding mouth to hers as her breasts squish out the top of her dress, but I can't concentrate. Metaphor leads me by the nose, into the maze, and suddenly all Eden lies before me. Porcupines, weasels, warthogs, and skunks, their feral gazes malicious or bland or stolid or piggy and sly. Agony, to see the romantic *frisson* quivering just out of reach, a dark-winged butterfly stuck to an overripe peach, and not to be able to swallow, or wallow. *Which one?* I murmur to the unresponding air. *Which one?*

THE
BOYS'
OWN
ANNUAL,
1911

was in my grandfather's attic, along with a pump
organ that contained bats, rafter-high piles of Western
paperbacks, and a dress form, my grandmother's
body frozen in wire when it still had a waist. The attic
smelled of dry rot and smoked eels but it had a
window, where the sunlight was yellower than anywhere else, because of the dust maybe. This buttery
sunlight framed the echoing African caves where
the underground streams ran, lightless, haunted by
crocodiles, white and eyeless, guarding the entrance
to the tunnel carved with Egyptian hieroglyphs and

armed with deadly snakes and spiky ambushes planted two thousand years ago to protect the chamber of the sacred pearl, which for some reason, in stories like this, was always black. And when the hero snatched it out of the stone forehead looming bulbous and idol-atrous there in the darkness, *filthy* was a word they liked, for other religions, the goddess was mad as blazes. Sinister priests with scimitars abounded, they could sniff you out like bloodhounds, their bare feet making no sound, until suddenly there was a set piece and down the hill went everyone, bounding along, loving it, yelling like crazy, bullets thudding into bodies into the scrub, into the surf, onto the waiting ship where Britain stood firm for plunder.

The issue with the last installment had never come; it wasn't in the attic. So there I was, suspended in mid-story, in 1951, and there I remain, sometime, waiting for the end, or finishing it off myself, in a book-lined London study over a stiff brandy, a yarn spun to a few choice gentlemen under the stuffed water buffalo head, a cheerful fire in the grate, or somewhere on the veldt, a bullet in the heart; who can tell where such greedy impulses will lead? Such lust for blind white crocodiles. In those times there were still chiefs in ostrich feathers and enemies worth killing, and loyalty, or so the story said. Through the attic window and its golden dust and flyhusks I could see the barn, unpainted, hay coming out like stuffing from the loft doorway, and around the corner of it my grandmother's cow. She'd hook you if she could, if you didn't have a pitchfork. She was sneaking up on someone invisible; possibly my half-uncle, gassed in the first war and never right since. The books had been his once.

STUMP
HUNTING

1.

Dead stumps are the favorite disguises of wild animals. How often have you been roaring past in your motorboat or paddling in your canoe when you've seen a dead stump sticking out of the water and said to yourself, *That looks like an animal*?

Just the head of course. Swimming.

And then when you came up to it, it was only a dead stump.

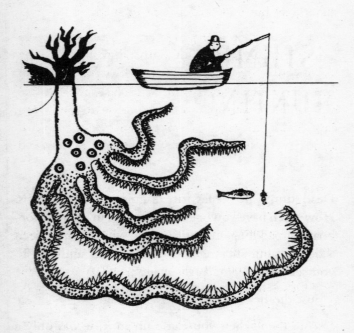

Don't be deceived! Usually these objects really are animals.

Here's what you do.

Shoot the animal, more or less between the eyes, or where you guess the eyes must be. This will kill the animal but will not cause it to shed its disguise.

The next task is getting the animal out of the water. This can be difficult, as the animal will still be holding on tenaciously with the parts of itself that look like roots. You may need a chainsaw, a lot of rope, and a powerful motor on your boat. When you have at last managed to chop and pry the animal loose, tow it to shore, where you will have parked your car.

No blood will be visible.

Let the animal dry out a little. It will be doing a good imitation of being waterlogged and very heavy. Heave it onto the hood of your car or the roof of your van and rope it down securely. Drive it into the city. Other hunters, with moose or bears or deer or even porcupines strapped to their own cars, will shake their heads and laugh at you, but remember: the last laugh will be yours.

When you get the animal home, butcher it in the back yard. Use the chainsaw again, and a diagram of a cow. The animal will still look like wood. But don't be fooled.

Wrap the steaks, ribs, and chops in freezer paper and put them in the freezer. If your wife questions what you are doing or makes disparaging remarks about your sanity, tell her to mind her own business. Conversely, quote from the Bible: *All flesh is grass.*

When you feel ready for a big meal of animal meat, take a steak from the freezer and heat up your charcoal or gas hibachi or your frying pan or grill. This is the moment at which the animal will be forced to reveal its true nature! Season the steak – we like a little barbecue sauce – and toss it onto the heat.

If it remains wood, you've made a mistake. Bad luck! You've picked the one dead stump out of a thousand that is not really an animal.

Try again later.

2.

The favorite disguise of fish is oval stones lying at the bottoms of streams.

MAKING
A MAN

This month we'll take a break from crocheted string bikinis and Leftovers Réchaufées to give our readers some tips on how to create, in their very own kitchens and rumpus rooms, an item that is both practical and decorative. It's nice to have one of these around the house, either out on the lawn looking busy, or propped in a chair, prone or erect. Choose the coverings to match the drapes!

When worn out, they can be re-covered and used as doorstops.

1. TRADITIONAL METHOD

Take some dust of the ground. Form. Breathe into the nostrils the breath of life. Simple, but effective!

(Please note that although men are made of dust, women are made of ribs. Remember that at your next Texas-style barbecue!)

Should you give your man a belly button, or not? Authorities on the traditional method disagree. We ourselves like to include one, as we think it adds a finishing touch. Use your thumb.

2. GINGERBREAD METHOD

Any good rolled-cookie recipe will do, but add extra ginger if you want lively results — and our readers who choose this method usually do! Raisins make good eyes and buttons, but you can use those little silver balls as long as you take care not to break your teeth on them.

Once your man has come out of your oven, you may have trouble hanging on to him. Men made this way are apt to take off down the road, on motorcycles or off them, robbing convenience stores, getting themselves tattooed, and hopping up and down and singing, 'Run, run, as fast as you can, you can't catch me, I'm the Gingerbread Man!' Attaching a string to his leg before the oven procedure may help, but – alas – in our experience, not for long.

There's one good thing to be said for this method, though these guys are scrumptious! Good enough to eat!

3. CLOTHES METHOD

Clothes make the man! How often have you heard it said?

Well, we couldn't agree more! However, clothes may make the man, but women – by and large – make the clothes, so it follows that the responsibility for the finished model lies with the home seamstress.

Use a good pattern and cut on the lines. Otherwise your man will be all screw-jiggy. Preshrink the fabric, or your man will turn out to be smaller than you'd hoped. Sew the darts first, and remember to give that tummy a good tuck, or you'll be sorry later!

Watch those zippers. A badly placed zipper can cause serious functional problems. It's fun to be different, but not too different!

Casual or formal is up to you; if in doubt, make two, and alternate. Be sure your house has a lot of mirrors. Men made this way – like budgies – seem to adore them!

One very creative woman we know sewed her entire man out of rubber sheeting. Then she used a bicycle pump. Amazing!

4.   MARZIPAN METHOD

We've often thought men would be easier to control if they were smaller. Well, here's a tiny rascal you can hold in the palm of your hand!

Usually found on wedding cakes, these formally dressed minigrooms require painstaking attention to detail, but it's worth the time you spend with the paintbrush and the food coloring to see the finished result smiling at you with deceptive blandness from the frothy topmost layer of Seven-Minute Boiled Icing!

We much regret the modern custom of substituting plastic for the original sugary confection. For one thing, there is absolutely no payoff when you feel the urge — as we do! — to pop one of these dapper devils into your mouth and suck off his clothes.

5. FOLK ART METHOD

You've seen these cuties in other folks' front yards, with little windmills attached to their heads. They hammer with their little hammers, saw with their little saws, or just whirl their arms around a lot when there's a stiff breeze. Alternatively, they may just stand stock-still, holding onto bridles, lanterns, or fishing poles. Some of them may be in gnome costumes.

Why shouldn't you concoct one of these cunning fellows for your very own? No reason at all! Just coat your hubby with plaster of Paris, and

MEN AT
SEA

You can come to the end of talking, about women, talking. In restaurants, cafés, kitchens, less frequently in bars or pubs, about relatives, relations, relationships, illnesses, jobs, children, men; about nuance, hunch, intimation, intuition, shadow; about themselves and each other; about what he said to her and she said to her and she said back; about what they feel.

Something more definite, more outward then, some action, to drain the inner swamp, sweep the inner fluff out from under the inner bed, harden the edges. Men at sea, for instance. Not on a submarine, too claustrophobic and smelly, but something more bracing, a tang of salt, cold water, all over your callused body, cuts and bruises, hurricanes, bravery, and above all no women. Women are replaced by water, by wind, by the ocean, shifting and treacherous; a man has to know what to do, to navigate, to sail, to bail, so reach for the how-to book, and out here it's what he said to him, or didn't say, a narrowing of the eyes, sizing the bastard up before the pounce, the knife to the gut, and here comes a wave, hang on to the shrouds, all teeth grit, all muscles bulge together. Or sneaking along the gangway, the passageway, the right of way, the Milky Way, in the dark, your eyes shining like digital wristwatches, and the bushes, barrels, scuppers, ditches, filthy with enemies, and you on the prowl for adrenaline and loot. Corpses of your own making deliquesce behind you as you reach the cave, abandoned city, safe, sliding panel, hole in the ground, and rich beyond your wildest dreams!

What now? Spend it on some woman, in a restaurant. And there I am, back again at the eternal table, which exists so she can put her elbows on it, over a glass of wine, while he says. What does he say? He says the story of how he got here, to her. She says, But what did you feel?

And his eyes roll wildly, quick as a wink he tries to think of something else, a cactus, a porpoise, never give yourself away, while the seductive waves swell the carpet beneath the feet and the wind freshens among the tablecloths. They're all around her, she can see it now, one per woman per table. Men, at sea.

SIMMERING

It started in the back yards. At first the men concentrated on heat and smoke, and on dangerous thrusts with long forks. Their wives gave them aprons in railroad stripes, with slogans on the front – HOT STUFF, THE BOSS – to spur them on. Then it began to get all mixed up with who should do the dishes, and you can't fall back on paper plates forever, and around that time the wives got tired of making butterscotch brownies and Jell-o salads with grated carrots and baby marshmallows in them and wanted to make money instead, and one thing led to another. The wives said that there were only twenty-four hours in a day; and the men, who in that century were still priding themselves on their rationality, had to agree that this was so.

For a while they worked it out that the men were in charge of the more masculine kinds of food: roasts, chops, steaks, dead chickens and ducks, gizzards, hearts, anything that had obviously been killed, that had visibly bled. The wives did the other things, the glazed parsnips and the prune whip, anything that flowered or fruited or was soft and gooey in the middle. That was all right for about a decade. Everyone praised the men to keep them going, and the wives, sneaking out of the houses in the mornings with their squeaky new briefcases, clutching their bus tickets because the men needed the station wagons to bring home the carcasses, felt they had got away with something.

But time is not static, and the men refused to stay put. They could not be kept isolated in their individual kitchens, kitchens into which the wives were allowed less and less frequently because, the men said, they did not sharpen the knives properly, if at all. The men began to acquire kitchen machines, which they would spend the weekends taking apart and oiling. There were a few accidents at first, a few lost fingers and ends of noses, but the men soon got the hang of it and branched out into other areas: automatic nutmeg graters, electric gadgets for taking the lids off jars. At cocktail parties they would gather in groups at one end of the room, exchanging private recipes and cooking yarns, tales of soufflés daringly saved at the last minute, pears flambées which had gone out of control and had to be fought to a standstill. Some of these stories had risqué phrases in them, such as *chicken breasts*. Indeed, sexual metaphor was changing: bowls and forks became prominent, and *eggbeater*, *pressure cooker*, and *turkey baster* became words which only the most daring young women, the kind who thought it was a kick to butter their own toast, would venture to pronounce in mixed company. Men who could not cook very well hung about the edges of these groups, afraid to say much, admiring the older and more experienced ones, wishing they could be like them.

Soon after that, the men resigned from their jobs in large numbers so they could spend more time in the kitchen. The magazines said it was a modern trend. The wives were all driven off to work, whether they wanted to or not: someone had to make the money, and of course they did not want their husbands' masculinity to be threatened. A man's status in the community was now displayed by the length of his carving knives, by how many of them he had and how sharp he kept them, and by whether they were plain or ornamented with gold and precious jewels.

Exclusive clubs and secret societies sprang up. Men meeting for the first time would now exchange special handshakes — the béchamel twist, the chocolate mousse double grip — to show that they had been initiated. It was pointed out to the women, who by this time did not go into the kitchens at all on pain of being thought unfeminine, that *chef* after all means *chief* and that Mixmasters were common but no one had ever heard of a Mixmistress. Psychological articles began to appear in the magazines on the origin of women's kitchen envy and how it could be cured. Amputation of the tip of the tongue was recommended, and, as you know, became a widespread practice in the more advanced nations. If Nature had meant women to cook, it was said, God would have made carving knives round and with holes in them.

This is history. But it is not a history familiar to

many people. It exists only in the few archival collections that have not yet been destroyed, and in manuscripts like this one, passed from woman to woman, usually at night, copied out by hand or memorized. It is subversive of me even to write these words. I am doing so, at the risk of my own personal freedom, because now, after so many centuries of stagnation, there are signs that hope and therefore change have once more become possible.

The women in their pinstripe suits, exiled to the living rooms, where they dutifully sip the glasses of port brought out to them by the men, used to sit uneasily, silently, listening to the loud bursts of male and somehow derisive laughter from behind the closed kitchen doors. But they have begun whispering to each other. When they are with those they trust, they tell of a time long ago, lost in the fogs of legend, hinted at in packets of letters found in attic trunks and in the cryptic frescoes on abandoned temple walls, when women too were allowed to participate in the ritual that now embodies the deepest religious convictions of our society: the transformation of the consecrated flour into the holy bread. At night they dream, long clandestine dreams, confused and obscured by shadows. They dream of plunging their hands into the earth, which is red as blood and soft, which is milky and warm. They dream that the earth gathers itself under their hands, swells, changes its form, flowers into a thousand shapes, for them too, for them once more. They dream of apples; they dream of the creation of the world; they dream of freedom.

HAPPY
ENDINGS

John and Mary meet.
What happens next?
If you want a happy ending, try A.

A. John and Mary fall in love and get married. They
    both have worthwhile and remunerative jobs
    which they find stimulating and challenging.
    They buy a charming house. Real estate values
    go up. Eventually, when they can afford live-in
    help, they have two children, to whom they are
    devoted. The children turn out well. John and

Mary have a stimulating and challenging sex life and worthwhile friends. They go on fun vacations together. They retire. They both have hobbies which they find stimulating and challenging. Eventually they die. This is the end of the story.

B. Mary falls in love with John but John doesn't fall in love with Mary. He merely uses her body for selfish pleasure and ego gratification of a tepid kind. He comes to her apartment twice a week and she cooks him dinner, you'll notice that he doesn't even consider her worth the price of a dinner out, and after he's eaten the dinner he fucks her and after that he falls asleep, while she does the dishes so he won't think she's untidy, having all those dirty dishes lying around, and puts on fresh lipstick so she'll look good when he wakes up, but when he wakes up he doesn't even notice, he puts on his socks and his shorts and his pants and his shirt and his tie and his shoes, the reverse order from the one in which he took them off. He doesn't take off Mary's clothes, she takes them off herself, she acts as if she's dying for it every time, not because she likes sex exactly, she doesn't, but she wants John to think she does because if they do it often enough surely he'll get used to her, he'll come to depend on her and they will get married, but John goes out the door with hardly so much as a goodnight and three days later he turns up at six o'clock and they do the whole thing over again.

Mary gets run down. Crying is bad for your face, everyone knows that and so does Mary but she can't stop. People at work notice. Her friends tell her John is a rat, a pig, a dog, he isn't good enough for her, but she can't believe it. Inside John, she thinks, is another John, who is much nicer. This other John will emerge like a butter-fly from a cocoon, a Jack from a box, a pit from a prune, if the first John is only squeezed enough.

One evening John complains about the food. He has never complained about the food before. Mary is hurt.

Her friends tell her they've seen him in a restaurant with another woman, whose name is Madge. It's not even Madge that finally gets to Mary; it's the restaurant. John has never taken

Mary to a restaurant. Mary collects all the sleeping pills and aspirins she can find, and takes them and half a bottle of sherry. You can see what kind of a woman she is by the fact that it's not even whiskey. She leaves a note for John. She hopes he'll discover her and get her to the hospital in time and repent and then they can get married, but this fails to happen and she dies.

John marries Madge and everything continues as in A.

C. John, who is an older man, falls in love with Mary, and Mary, who is only twenty-two, feels sorry for him because he's worried about his hair falling out. She sleeps with him even though she's not in love with him. She met him at work. She's in love with someone called James, who is twenty-two also and not yet ready to settle down.

John on the contrary settled down long ago: this is what is bothering him. John has a steady respectable job and is getting ahead in his field, but Mary isn't impressed by him, she's impressed by James, who has a motorcycle and a fabulous record collection. But James is often away on his motorcycle, being free. Freedom isn't the same for girls, so in the meantime Mary spends Thursday evenings with John. Thursdays are the only days John can get away.

John is married to a woman called Madge and they have two children, a charming house which they bought just before the real estate values went up, and hobbies which they find stimulating and challenging, when they have the time. John tells Mary how important she is to him, but of course he can't leave his wife because a commitment is a commitment. He goes on about this more than is necessary and Mary finds it boring, but older men can keep it up longer so on the whole she has a fairly good time.

One day James breezes in on his motorcycle with some top-grade California hybrid and James and Mary get higher than you'd believe possible and they climb into bed. Everything becomes very underwater, but along comes John, who has a key to Mary's apartment. He finds them stoned and entwined. He's hardly in any position to be jealous, considering Madge, but nevertheless he's overcome with despair. Finally he's middle-aged, in two years he'll be bald as an egg, and he can't stand it. He purchases a handgun, saying he needs it for target practice – this is the thin part of the plot, but it can be dealt with later – and shoots the two of them and himself.

Madge, after a suitable period of mourning, marries an understanding man called Fred and everything continues as in A, but under different names.

D. Fred and Madge have no problems. They get along exceptionally well and are good at working out any little difficulties that may arise. But their charming house is by the seashore and one day a giant tidal wave approaches. Real estate values go down. The rest of the story is about what caused the tidal wave and how they escape from it. They do, though thousands drown. Some of the story is about how the thousands drown, but Fred and Madge are virtuous and lucky. Finally on high ground they clasp each other, wet and dripping and grateful, and continue as in A.

E. Yes, but Fred has a bad heart. The rest of the story is about how kind and understanding they both are until Fred dies. Then Madge devotes herself to charity work until the end of A. If you like, it can be 'Madge,' 'cancer,' 'guilty and confused,' and 'bird watching.'

F. If you think this is all too bourgeois, make John a revolutionary and Mary a counterespionage agent and see how far that gets you. Remember, this is Canada. You'll still end up with A, though in between you may get a lustful brawling saga of passionate involvement, a chronicle of our times, sort of.

You'll have to face it, the endings are the same however you slice it. Don't be deluded by any other endings, they're all fake, either deliberately fake, with malicious intent to deceive, or just motivated by excessive optimism if not by down-right sentimentality.

The only authentic ending is the one provided here:

John and Mary die. John and Mary die. John and Mary die.

So much for endings. Beginnings are always more fun. True connoisseurs, however, are known to favor the stretch in between, since it's the hardest to do anything with.

That's about all that can be said for plots, which anyway are just one thing after another, a what and a what and a what.

Now try How and Why.

LET US
NOW
PRAISE
STUPID
WOMEN

– the airheads, the bubblebrains, the ditzy blondes:
the headstrong teenagers too dumb to listen to their
    mothers:
all those with mattress stuffing between their ears,
all the lush hostesses who tell us to have a good day
    and give us the wrong change while checking
    their Big Hair in the mirror,
all those who dry their freshly shampooed poodles in
    the microwave,
and those whose boyfriends tell them chlorophyll
    chewing gum is a contraceptive, and who believe
    it;

all those with nervously bitten fingernails because they don't know whether to pee or get off the pot,

all those who don't know how to spell the word *pee*,

all those who laugh good-naturedly at stupid jokes like this one, even though they don't get the point.

They don't live in the real world, we tell ourselves fondly: but what kind of criticism is that?

If they can manage not to live in it, good for them. We would rather not live in it either, ourselves.

And in fact they don't live in it, because such women are fictions: composed by others, but just as frequently by themselves,

though even stupid women are not so stupid as they pretend: they pretend for love.

Men love them because they make even stupid men feel smart: women for the same reason,

and because they are reminded of all the stupid things they have done themselves,

but mostly because without them there would be no stories.

No stories! No stories! Imagine a world without stories!

But that's exactly what you would have, if all the
women were wise.
The Wise Virgins keep their lamps trimmed and
filled with oil, and the bridegroom arrives, in the
proper way, knocking at the front door, in time
for his dinner;
no fuss, no muss, and also no story at all.
What can be told about the Wise Virgins, such
bloodless paragons?
They bite their tongues, they watch their smart
mouths, they sew their own clothing,
they achieve professional recognition, they do every
right thing without effort.
Somehow they are insupportable: they have no
narrative vices:
their wise smiles are too knowing, too knowing
about us and our stupidities.
We suspect them of having mean hearts.
They are far too clever, not for their own good but
for ours.

The Foolish Virgins, on the other hand, let their
lamps go out:
and when the bridegroom turns up and rings the
doorbell,

they are asleep in bed, and he has to climb in
   through the window:
and people scream and fall over things, and identities
   get mistaken,
and there's a chase scene, and breakage, and much
   satisfactory uproar:
none of which would have happened if these girls
   hadn't been several bricks short of a load.

• • •

Ah the Eternal Stupid Woman! How we enjoy
   hearing about her:
as she listens to the con-artist yarns of the plausible
   snake,
and ends up eating the free sample of the apple from
   the Tree of Knowledge:
thus giving birth to Theology;
or as she opens the tricky gift box containing all
   human evils,
but is stupid enough to believe that Hope will be
   some kind of a solace.

She talks with wolves, without knowing what sort of
   beasts they are:
Where have you been all my life? they ask. *Where have
   I been all my life?* she replies.

We know! *We* know! And we know wolfishness
   when we see it!
Look out, we shout at her silently, thinking of all the
   smart things we would do in her place.
But trapped inside the white pages, she can't hear us,
and goes prancing and warbling and lolloping inno-
   cently towards her doom.
(Innocence! Perhaps that's the key to stupidity,
we tell ourselves, who think we gave it up long ago.)
If she escapes from anything, it's by sheer luck, or
   else the hero:
this girl couldn't tear her way out of a paper bag.

• • •

Sometimes she's stupidly fearless; on the other hand,
she can be just as equally fearful, though stupidly so.
Incest-minded stepfathers chase her through ruined
   cloisters,
where she's been lured by ruses too transparent to
   fool a gerbil.
Mice make her scream: she whimpers, teeth chatter-
   ing, through the menacing world,
running – but running involves legs, and is graceless
   – fleeing, rather.
Leglessly she flees, taking the wrong turn at every
   turn,

a white chiffon scarf in the darkness, and we flee
    with her.
Orphaned and minus kind aunts, she makes in-
    appropriate marital choices,
and has to dodge ropes, knives, crazed dogs, stone
    flower urns toppled off balconies,
aimed at her jittery head by suave, evil husbands out
    for her cash and blood.
Don't feel sorry for her, as she stands there helplessly
    wringing her hands:
fear is her armor.

Let's face it, she's our inspiration! The Muse as
    fluffball!
And the inspiration of men, as well! Why else were
    the sagas of heroes,
of their godlike strength and superhuman exploits,
    ever composed,
if not for the admiration of women thought stupid
    enough to believe them?
Where did five hundred years of love lyrics come
    from,
not to mention those plaintive imploring songs, all
    musical whines and groans?
Aimed straight at women stupid enough to find
    them seductive!

When lovely woman stoops or bungles her way into
    folly,
pleading her good intentions, her wish to please,
and is taken advantage of, especially by somebody
    famous,
if stupid or smart enough, she gets caught, just as in
    classic novels,
and makes her way into the tabloids, confused and
    tearful,
and from there straight into our hearts.
We forgive you! we cry. *We understand! Now do it some
    more!*

Hypocrite lecteuse! Ma semblable! Ma soeur!
Let us now praise stupid women,
who have given us Literature.

THE
VICTORY
BURLESK

I went to the Victory Burlesk twice, or maybe it was only once and one of my friends went the other time and told me about it. I enjoyed it both times. It was considered quite daring for young women to go to such a place, and we thought it was funny; it was almost as funny as church.

You got a stand-up comic, a movie, and a man who sang or juggled plates, as well as the striptease act. They used a lot of colored lighting, red and blue and purple. Each girl had a fake name: Miss Take, Miss Behave, Flame LeRew. I liked the names and the costumes, for their ingenuity, and I liked the more skillful girls, the ones who could twirl tassles or make their bellies or buttocks rotate in a circle. That was before they had to take it all off, there was an art to it, it was almost like the plate juggling. I liked the way they floated in the pools of colored light, moving as if they were swimming, mermaids behind glass.

One woman began with her back to the audience, the spotlight on her. She was wearing long white gloves and a black evening gown with gauzy black sleeves that looked like membranous wings as she stretched out her arms. She did a lot with her arms and back; but when she finally turned around, she was old. Her face was powdered dead white, her mouth was a bright reddish purple, but she was old. I could feel shame washing through me, it was no longer funny, I didn't want this woman to take off her clothes, I didn't want to look. I felt that I, not the woman on the stage, was being exposed and humiliated. Surely they would jeer and yell things at her, surely they would feel they had been tricked.

The woman unzipped her black evening gown, slipping it down, and began to move her hips. She smiled with her white mask of a face and her purple mouth, inside her lips her teeth glinted, dull white pebbles, it was a mockery, she didn't intend it, she knew it, it was a trick of another kind but we didn't know who was playing it. The trick was that suddenly there was no trick: the body up there was actual, it was aging, it was not floating in the spotlight somewhere apart from us, like us it was caught in time.

The Victory Burlesk went dead. Nobody made a sound.

SHE

knows exactly what she's doing. Well, why not?
Along the street, around the corner, the piece of her
that's just disappearing. If that's the way it works,
that's what she'll do. Sometimes in shorts, with
tanned thighs, or with sleeves like cabbages, or the
whole body falling liquid from the shoulders: whatever's about to happen. Lace at the throat, the ankle,
skimming the breasts, wherever they're putting it this
year, and a laugh or not, at the pulsepoint. What will
it get her? Something. You have to know when to
run and where, how to close a door, gently. Just a

little showing, something that looks like flesh, they follow, a few white stones dropped in the forest, under the trees, shining in the moonlight, clues, a trail. To get from one point to the next and then see another, and another beyond that. She deals in longing, the sickness of the heart, stuttering of the arteries, would you call it suffering, where does it lead? Deeper into the forest, deeper into the moonlight. They think they'll come out from among the trees and she will be there, finally waiting, for them, all cool white light.

THE
FEMALE
BODY

' . . . entirely devoted to the subject of "The Female Body." Knowing how well you have written on this topic . . . this capacious topic . . . '
– letter from the *Michigan Quarterly Review*

1.

I agree, it's a hot topic. But only one? Look around, there's a wide range. Take my own, for instance.

I get up in the morning. My topic feels like hell.

I sprinkle it with water, brush parts of it, rub it with towels, powder it, add lubricant. I dump in the fuel and away goes my topic, my topical topic, my controversial topic, my capacious topic, my limping topic, my nearsighted topic, my topic with back problems, my badly behaved topic, my vulgar topic, my outrageous topic, my aging topic, my topic that is out of the question and anyway still can't spell, in its oversized coat and worn winter boots, scuttling along the sidewalk as if it were flesh and blood, hunting for what's out there, an avocado, an alderman, an adjective, hungry as ever.

2.

The basic Female Body comes with the following accessories: garter belt, panty girdle, crinoline, camisole, bustle, brassiere, stomacher, chemise, virgin zone, spike heels, nose ring, veil, kid gloves, fishnet stockings, fichu, bandeau, Merry Widow, weepers, chokers, barrettes, bangles, beads, lorgnette, feather boa, basic black, compact, Lycra stretch one-piece with modesty panel, designer peignoir, flannel nightie, lace teddy, bed, head.

3.

The Female Body is made of transparent plastic and lights up when you plug it in. You press a button to illuminate the different systems. The Circulatory System is red, for the heart and arteries, purple for the veins; the Respiratory System is blue, the Lymphatic System is yellow, the Digestive System is green, with liver and kidneys in aqua. The nerves are done in orange and the brain is pink. The skeleton, as you might expect, is white.

The Reproductive System is optional, and can be removed. It comes with or without a miniature embryo. Parental judgment can thereby be exercised. We do not wish to frighten or offend.

4.

He said, I won't have one of those things in the house. It gives a young girl a false notion of beauty, not to mention anatomy. If a real woman was built like that she'd fall on her face.

She said, If we don't let her have one like all the

other girls she'll feel singled out. It'll become an issue. She'll long for one and she'll long to turn into one. Repression breeds sublimation. You know that.

He said, It's not just the pointy plastic tits, it's the wardrobes. The wardrobes and that stupid male doll, what's his name, the one with the underwear glued on.

She said, Better to get it over with when she's young. He said, All right but don't let me see it.

She came whizzing down the stairs, thrown like a dart. She was stark naked. Her hair had been chopped off, her head was turned back to front, she was missing some toes and she'd been tattooed all over her body with purple ink, in a scrollwork design. She hit the potted azalea, trembled there for a moment like a botched angel, and fell.

He said, I guess we're safe.

5.

The Female Body has many uses. It's been used as a door knocker, a bottle-opener, as a clock with a ticking belly, as something to hold up lampshades, as a nutcracker, just squeeze the brass legs together and out comes your nut. It bears torches, lifts victorious wreaths, grows copper wings and raises aloft a ring of neon stars; whole buildings rest on its marble heads.

It sells cars, beer, shaving lotion, cigarettes, hard liquor; it sells diet plans and diamonds, and desire in tiny crystal bottles. Is this the face that launched a thousand products? You bet it is, but don't get any funny big ideas, honey, that smile is a dime a dozen.

It does not merely sell, it is sold. Money flows into this country or that country, flies in, practically crawls in, suitful after suitful, lured by all those hairless preteen legs. Listen, you want to reduce the national debt, don't you? Aren't you patriotic? That's the spirit. That's my girl.

She's a natural resource, a renewable one luckily, because those things wear out so quickly. They don't make 'em like they used to. Shoddy goods.

6.

One and one equals another one. Pleasure in the female is not a requirement. Pair-bonding is stronger in geese. We're not talking about love, we're talking about biology. That's how we all got here, daughter.

Snails do it differently. They're hermaphrodites, and work in threes.

7.

Each female body contains a female brain. Handy. Makes things work. Stick pins in it and you get amazing results. Old popular songs. Short circuits. Bad dreams.

Anyway: each of these brains has two halves. They're joined together by a thick cord; neural pathways flow from one to the other, sparkles of electric information washing to and fro. Like light on waves. Like a conversation. How does a woman know? She listens. She listens in.

The male brain, now, that's a different matter. Only a thin connection. Space over here, time over there, music and arithmetic in their own sealed compartments. The right brain doesn't know what the left brain is doing. Good for aiming though, for hitting the target when you pull the trigger. What's the target? Who's the target? Who cares? What matters is hitting it. That's the male brain for you. Objective.

This is why men are so sad, why they feel so cut off, why they think of themselves as orphans cast adrift, footloose and stringless in the deep void. What void? she says. What are you talking about? The void of the Universe, he says, and she says Oh and looks out the window and tries to get a handle on it, but it's no use, there's too much going on, too many rustlings in the leaves, too many voices, so she says, Would you like a cheese sandwich, a piece of cake, a cup of tea? And he grinds his teeth because she doesn't understand, and wanders off, not just alone but Alone, lost in the dark, lost in the skull, searching for the other half, the twin who could complete him.

Then it comes to him: he's lost the Female Body! Look, it shines in the gloom, far ahead, a vision of wholeness, ripeness, like a giant melon, like an apple, like a metaphor for *breast* in a bad sex novel; it shines like a balloon, like a foggy noon, a watery moon, shimmering in its egg of light.

Catch it. Put it in a pumpkin, in a high tower, in a compound, in a chamber, in a house, in a room. Quick, stick a leash on it, a lock, a chain, some pain, settle it down, so it can never get away from you again.

COLD-
BLOODED

To my sisters, the Iridescent Ones, the Egg-Bearers, the Many-Faceted, greetings from the Planet of Moths.

At last we have succeeded in establishing contact with the creatures here who, in their ability to communicate, to live in colonies, and to construct technologies, most resemble us, although in these particulars they have not advanced above a rudimentary level.

During our first observation of these 'blood creatures,' as we have termed them – after the colorful

red liquid that is to be found inside their bodies, and that appears to be of great significance to them in their poems, wars, and religious rituals – we supposed them incapable of speech, as those specimens we were able to examine entirely lacked the organs for it. They had no wing casings with which to stribulate – indeed they had no wings; they had no mandibles to click; and the chemical method was unknown to them, since they were devoid of antennae. 'Smell,' for them, is a perfunctory affair, confined to a flattened and numbed appendage on the front of the head. But after a time, we discovered that the incoherent squeakings and gruntings that emerged from them, especially when pinched, were in fact a form of language, and after that we made rapid progress.

We soon ascertained that their planet, named by us the Planet of Moths after its most prolific and noteworthy genus, is called by these creatures *Earth*. They have some notion that their ancestors were created from this substance; or so it is claimed in many of their charming but irrational folktales.

In an attempt to establish common ground, we asked them at what season they mated with and then devoured their males. Imagine our embarrassment when we discovered that those individuals with whom we were conversing *were* males! (It is very hard to tell the difference, as their males are not diminutive, as ours are, but if anything bigger. Also, lacking natural beauty — brilliantly patterned carapaces, diaphanous wings, luminescent eyes, and the like — they attempt to imitate our kind by placing upon their bodies various multicolored draperies, which conceal their generative parts.)

We apologized for our faux pas, and inquired as to their own sexual practices. Picture our nausea and disgust when we discovered that it is the male, not the egg-bearer, which is the most prized among them! Abnormal as this will seem to you, my sisters, their leaders are for the most part male; which may account for their state of relative barbarism. Another peculiarity which must be noted is that, although they frequently kill them in many other ways, they rarely devour their females after procreation. This is a waste of protein; but then, they are a wasteful people.

We hastily abandoned this painful subject.

Next we asked them when they pupated. Here again, as in the case of 'clothing' — the draperies we have mentioned — we uncovered a fumbling attempt at imitation of our kind. At some indeterminate point in their life cycles, they cause themselves to be placed in artificial stone or wooden cocoons, or chrysalises. They have an idea that they will some-day emerge from these in an altered state, which they symbolize with carvings of themselves with wings. However, we did not observe that any had actually done so.

It is as well to mention at this juncture that in addition to the many species of moths for which it is justly famous among us, the Planet of Moths abounds in thousands of varieties of creatures which resemble our own distant ancestors. It seems that one of our previous attempts at colonization – an attempt so distant that our record of it is lost – must have borne fruit. However, these beings, although numerous and ingenious, are small in size and primi-tive in their social organization, and attempts to communicate with them were not – or have not been, so far – very successful. The blood creatures are hostile towards them, and employ against them many poisonous sprays, traps, and so forth, in addition to a sinister manual device termed a 'fly swatter.' It is agonizing indeed to watch one of these instruments of torture and death being wielded by the large and frenzied against the small and helpless;

but the rules of diplomacy forbid our intervention. (Luckily the blood creatures cannot understand what we say to one another about them in our own language.)

But despite all the machinery of destruction that is aimed at them, our distant relatives are more than holding their own. They feed on the crops and herd animals and even on the flesh of the blood creatures; they live in their homes, devour their clothes, hide and flourish in the very cracks of their floors. When the blood creatures have succeeded at last in over-breeding themselves, as it seems their intention to do, or in exterminating one another, rest assured that our kind, already superior in both numbers and adaptability, will be poised to achieve the ascendency that is ours by natural right.

This will not happen tomorrow, but it will happen. As you know, my sisters, we have long been a patient race.

LIKING
MEN

It's time to like men again. Where shall we begin?

I have a personal preference for the backs of necks, because of the word *nape*, so lightly furred; which is different from the word *scruff*. But for most of us, especially the beginners, it's best to start with the feet and work up. To begin with the head and all it contains would be too suddenly painful. Then there's the navel, birth dimple, where we fell from the stem, something we have in common; you could look at it and say, *He also is mortal.* But it may be too close for comfort to those belts and zippers which cause you such distress, and comfort is what you want. He's a carnivore, you're a vegetarian. That's what you have to get over.

The feet then. I give you the feet, pinkly toed and innocuous. Unfortunately you think of socks, lying on the floor, waiting to be picked up and washed. Quickly add shoes. Better? The socks are now contained, and presumably clean.

You contemplate the shoes, shined but not too much – you don't want this man to be either a messy slob or prissy – and you begin to relax. Shoes, kind and civilized, not black but a decent shade of brown. No raucous two-tones, no elevator heels. The shoes dance, with the feet in them, neatly, adroitly, you enjoy this, you think of Fred Astaire, you're beginning to like men. You think of kissing those feet, slowly, after a good scrubbing of course; the feet expand their toes, squirm with pleasure. You like to give pleasure. You run your tongue along the sole and the feet moan.

Cheered up, you start fooling around. *Footgear*, you think. Golf shoes, grassy and fatherly, white sneakers for playing tennis in, agile and sweet, quick as rabbits. Workboots, solid and trustworthy. A good man is hard to find but they do exist, you know it now. Someone who can run a chainsaw without cutting off his leg. What a relief. Checks and plaids, laconic, a little Scottish. Rubber boots, for wading out to the barn in the rain in order to save the baby calf. Power, quiet and sane. Knowing what to do, doing it well. Sexy.

But rubber boots aren't the only kind. You don't want to go on but you can't stop yourself. Riding boots, you think, with the sinister crop; but that's not too bad, they're foreign and historical. Cowboy boots, two of them, planted apart, stomp, stomp, on Main Street just before the shot rings out. A spur, in the groin. A man's gotta do, but why this? Jackboots, so highly shined you can see your own face in the right one, as the left one raises itself and the heel comes down on your nose. Now you see rows of them, marching, marching; yours is the street-level view, because you are lying down. Power is the power to smash, two hold your legs, two your arms, the fifth shoves a pointed instrument into you; a bayonet, the neck of a broken bottle, and it's not even wartime, this is a park, with a children's playground, tiny red and yellow horses, it's daytime, men and women stare at you out of their closed car windows. Later the policeman will ask you what you did to provoke this. Boots were not such a bright idea after all.

But just because all rapists are men it doesn't follow that all men are rapists, you tell yourself. You try desperately to retain the image of the man you love and also like, but now it's a sand-colored plain, no houses left standing anywhere, columns of smoke ascending, trenches filled with no quarter, heads with the faces rotting away, mothers, babies, young boys and girls, men as well, turning to skulls, who did this? Who defines *enemy?* How can you like men?

Still, you continue to believe it can be done. If not all men, at least some, at least two, at least one. It takes an act of faith. There is his foot, sticking out from under the sheet, asleep, naked as the day he was born. The day he was born. Maybe that's what you have to go back to, in order to trace him here, the journey he took, step by step. In order to begin. Again and again.

IN LOVE
WITH
RAYMOND
CHANDLER

An affair with Raymond Chandler, what a joy! Not because of the mangled bodies and the marinated cops and hints of eccentric sex, but because of his interest in furniture. He knew that furniture could breathe, could feel, not as we do but in a way more muffled, like the word *upholstery*, with its overtones of mustiness and dust, its bouquet of sunlight on aging cloth or of scuffed leather on the backs and seats of sleazy office chairs. I think of his sofas, stuffed to roundness, satin-covered, pale blue like the eyes of his cold blond unbodied murderous women, beating very slowly, like the hearts of hibernating crocodiles; of his chaises longues, with their malicious pillows. He knew about front lawns too, and greenhouses, and the interiors of cars.

This is how our love affair would go. We would meet at a hotel, or a motel, whether expensive or cheap it wouldn't matter. We would enter the room, lock the door, and begin to explore the furniture, fingering the curtains, running our hands along the spurious gilt frames of the pictures, over the real marble or the chipped enamel of the luxurious or tacky washroom sink, inhaling the odor of the carpets, old cigarette smoke and spilled gin and fast meaningless sex or else the rich abstract scent of the oval transparent soaps imported from England, it wouldn't matter to us; what would matter would be our response to the furniture, and the furniture's response to us. Only after we had sniffed, fingered, rubbed, rolled on, and absorbed the furniture of the room would we fall into each other's arms, and onto the bed (king-size? peach-colored? creaky? narrow? four-posted? pioneer-quilted? lime-green chenille-covered?), ready at last to do the same things to each other.

SIMPLE
MURDERS

He had a thin rapacious mustache and very pointed shoes. She had green eyes and hair the color of flame. He had a silver cigarette case and large, brutal thumbs. She had a scar across her cheekbone and a bitter laugh. He had the guileless blue eyes of a cherub but the soulless smile of a fiend. She had a black hat. He had a black cat. Every single one of them was in disguise.

• • •

He was lying face down on the priceless oriental carpet, with the bejeweled handle of the dagger protruding from between his expensively suited shoulder blades. She was draped over the disheveled bed in her red nylon negligee, with the livid marks of ten huge fingers standing out on her throat.

No. Let's start again.

He was sheathed in green plastic garbage bags, tied neatly all the way down with a row of his own festive neckties, and buried at the bottom of the garden. They never would have found him if the neighbor hadn't wanted to replace the fence. It was the wife who did it, with a frying pan. He'd been beating her up for years.

As for the other one, she was run through a meat grinder and frozen in little freezer baggies labeled 'Stew.' Her daughter wanted the old-age checks. I learned about all of this in a British Rail station, en route to Norwich, because my train was late. You can't make such things up.

• • •

It was because of the chocolate bars. It was because of the stars. It was because of a life behind bars. It was her hormones. It was the radiation from the wires and phones. It was his mother saying, *You'll never amount to a hill of beans.* It was because he was so all-fired mean. It was the sleeping pills. It was the frills, on the blouse, under the jacket, over the breasts. It was the blood tests. It was the sigh, the cry, the hand on the thigh. It was the hunger, it was the rage, it was the spirit of the age.

It was a coincidence. It was the wrong bottle. My hand slipped. How was I to know it was loaded?

It was the fear. It was the cold, cold voice of the frozen angel, the voice from the outer darkness, whispering in my ear.

• • •

Mr. Plum, in the conservatory, with the wrench. She saw the wrench and she said, *What's that wrench for?* And I thought she wanted sex. So I strangled her.

• • •

It was the dog hair on the back seat of the car. It was the bloodstain on the chandelier. It was the finger-nail in the pail. It was the chalice with the palace. It was the chicken that did nothing in the nighttime. It was the one detail you always forget, and for that they will come to get you. *Aha*, they will say. *You thought you were so smart.* This is the worst part, just before you wake.

• • •

It was the heart, the too-small heart, the too-small devious heart, the lopsided heart, the impoverished heart, the heart someone dropped, the heart with a crack in it. It was the heart that thought it needed to kill. To show them all. To feel. To heal. To become whole.

ICONOGRAPHY

He wants her arranged just so. He wants her, arranged. He arranges to want her.

This is the arrangement they have made. With strings attached, or ropes, stockings, leather straps. What else is arranged? Furniture, flowers. For contemplation and a graceful disposition of parts to compose a unified and aesthetic whole.

Once she wasn't supposed to like it. To have her in a position she didn't like, that was power. Even if she liked it she had to pretend she didn't. Then she was supposed to like it. To make her do something she didn't like and then make her like it, that was greater power. The greatest power of all is when she doesn't really like it but she's supposed to like it, so she has to pretend.

Whether he's making her like it or making her dislike it or making her pretend to like it is important, but it's not the most important thing. The most important thing is making her. Over, from nothing, new. From scratch, the way he wants.

It can never be known whether she likes it or not. By this time she doesn't know herself. All you see is the skin, that smile of hers, flat but indelible, like a tattoo. Hard to tell, and she never will, she can't. They don't get into it unless they like it, he says. He has the last word. He has the word.

Watch yourself. That's what the mirrors are for, this story is a mirror story which rhymes with horror story, almost but not quite. We fall back into these rhythms as if into safe hands.

ALIEN TERRITORY

1.

He conceives himself in alien territory. Not his turf – alien! Listen! The rushing of the red rivers, the rustling of the fresh leaves in the dusk, always in the dusk, under the dark stars, and the wish-wash, wish-wash of the heavy soothing sea, which becomes – yes! – the drums of the natives, beating, beating, louder, faster, lower, slower. Are they hostile? Who knows, because they're invisible.

He sleeps and wakes, wakes and sleeps, and suddenly all is movement and suffering and terror and

he is shot out gasping for breath into blinding light and a place that's even more dangerous, where food is scarce and two enormous giants stand guard over his wooden prison. Shout as he might, rattle the bars, nobody comes to let him out. One of the giants is boisterous and hair-covered, with a big stick; the other walks more softly but has two enormous bulgy comforts which she selfishly refuses to detach and give away, to him. Neither of them looks anything like him, and their language is incomprehensible.

Aliens! What can he do? And to make it worse, they surround him with animals — bears, rabbits, cats, giraffes — each one of them stuffed and, evidently, castrated, because although he looks and looks, all they have at best is a tail. Is this the fate the aliens have in store for him, as well?

Where did I come from? he asks, for what will not be the first time. *Out of me*, the bulgy one says fondly, as if he should be pleased. Out of *where?* Out of *what?* He covers his ears, shutting out the untruth, the shame, the pulpy horror. It is not to be thought, it is not to be borne!

No wonder that at the first opportunity he climbs out the window and joins a gang of other explorers, each one of them an exile, an immigrant, like himself. Together they set out on their solitary journeys.

What are they searching for? Their homeland. Their true country. The place they came from, which can't possibly be here.

2.

All men are created equal, as someone said who was either very hopeful or very mischievous. What a lot of anxiety could have been avoided if he'd only kept his mouth shut.

Sigmund was wrong about the primal scene: Mom and Dad, keyhole version. That might be upsetting, true, but there's another one:

Five guys standing outside, pissing into a snowbank, a river, the underbrush, pretending not to look down. Or maybe *not* looking down: gazing upward, at the stars, which gives us the origin of astronomy. Anything to avoid comparisons, which aren't so much odious as intimidating.

And not only astronomy: quantum physics, engineering, laser technology, all numeration between zero and infinity. Something safely abstract, detached from you; a transfer of the obsession with size to anything at all. Lord, Lord, they measure everything: the height of the Great Pyramids, the rate of fingernail growth, the multiplication of viruses, the sands of the sea, the number of angels that can dance on the head of a pin. And then it's only a short step to proving that God is a mathematical equation. Not a person. Not a body, Heaven forbid. Not one like yours. Not an earthbound one, not one with size and therefore pain.

When you're feeling blue, just keep on whistling. Just keep on measuring. Just don't look down.

3.

The history of war is a history of killed bodies. That's what war is: bodies killing other bodies, bodies being killed.

Some of the killed bodies are those of women and children, as a side effect, you might say. Fallout, shrapnel, napalm, rape and skewering, antipersonnel devices. But most of the killed bodies are men. So are most of those doing the killing.

Why do men want to kill the bodies of other men? Women don't want to kill the bodies of other women. By and large. As far as we know.

Here are some traditional reasons: Loot. Territory. Lust for power. Hormones. Adrenaline high. Rage. God. Flag. Honor. Righteous anger. Revenge. Oppression. Slavery. Starvation. Defense of one's life. Love; or, a desire to protect the women and children. From what? From the bodies of other men.

What men are most afraid of is not lions, not snakes, not the dark, not women. Not any more. What men are most afraid of is the body of another man.

Men's bodies are the most dangerous things on earth.

4.

On the other hand, it could be argued that men don't have any bodies at all. Look at the magazines! Magazines for women have women's bodies on the covers, magazines for men have women's bodies on the covers. When men appear on the covers of magazines, it's magazines about money, or about world news. Invasions, rocket launches, political coups, interest rates, elections, medical breakthroughs. *Reality*. Not *entertainment*. Such magazines show only the heads, the unsmiling heads, the talking heads, the decision-making heads, and maybe a little glimpse, a coy flash of suit. How do we know there's a body, under all that discreet pinstriped tailoring? We don't, and maybe there isn't.

What does this lead us to suppose? That women are bodies with heads attached, and men are heads with bodies attached? Or not, depending.

You can have a body, though, if you're a rock star, an athlete, or a gay model. As I said, *entertainment*. Having a body is not altogether serious.

5.

Or else too serious for words.

The thing is: men's bodies aren't dependable. Now it does, now it doesn't, and so much for the triumph of the will. A man is the puppet of his body, or vice versa. He and it make tomfools of each other;

it lets him down. Or up, at the wrong moment. Just stare hard out the schoolroom window and recite the multiplication tables, and pretend this isn't happening! Your face at least can be immobile. Easier to have a trained dog, which will do what you want it to, nine times out of ten.

The other thing is: men's bodies are detachable. Consider the history of statuary: the definitive bits get knocked off so easily, through revolution or prudery or simple transportation, with leaves stuck on for substitutes, fig or grape; or, in more northern climates, maple. A man and his body are soon parted.

In the old old days, you became a man through blood. Through incisions, tattoos, splinters of wood; through an intimate wound, and the refusal to flinch. Through being beaten by older boys, in the dormitory, with a wooden paddle you were forced to carve yourself. The torments varied, but they were all torments. *It's a boy*, they cry with joy. *Let's cut some off!*

Every morning I get down on my knees and thank God for not creating me a man. A man so chained to unpredictability. A man so much at the mercy of himself. A man so prone to sadness. A man who has to take it like a man. A man, who can't fake it.

In the gap between desire and enactment, noun and verb, intention and infliction, *want* and *have*, compassion begins.

6.

Bluebeard ran off with the third sister, intelligent though beautiful, and shut her up in his palace. *Everything here is yours, my dear*, he said to her. *Just don't open the small door. I will give you the key, however. I expect you not to use it.*

Believe it or not, this sister was in love with him, even though she knew he was a serial killer. She roamed over the whole palace, ignoring the jewels and the silk dresses and the piles of gold. Instead she went through the medicine cabinet and the kitchen drawers, looking for clues to his uniqueness. Because she loved him, she wanted to understand him. She also wanted to cure him. She thought she had the healing touch.

But she didn't find out a lot. In his closet there

were suits and ties and matching shoes and casual wear, some golf outfits and a tennis racquet, and some jeans for when he wanted to rake up the leaves. Nothing unusual, nothing kinky, nothing sinister. She had to admit to being a little disappointed.

She found his previous women quite easily. They were in the linen closet, neatly cut up and ironed flat and folded, stored in mothballs and lavender. Bachelors acquire such domestic skills. The women didn't make much of an impression on her, except the one who looked like his mother. That one she took out with rubber gloves on and slipped into the incinerator in the garden. *Maybe it was his mother*, she thought. *If so, good riddance.*

She read through his large collection of cook-books, and prepared the dishes on the most-thumbed pages. At dinner he was politeness itself, pulling out her chair and offering more wine and leading the conversation around to topics of the day. She said gently that she wished he would talk more about his feelings. He said that if she had his feelings, she wouldn't want to talk about them either. This intrigued her. She was now more in love with him and more curious than ever.

Well, she thought, *I've tried everything else; it's the small door or nothing. Anyway, he gave me the key.* She waited until he had gone to the office or wherever it was he went, and made straight for the small door. When she opened it, what should be inside but a dead child. A small dead child, with its eyes wide open.

It's mine, he said, coming up behind her. *I gave birth to it. I warned you. Weren't you happy with me?*

It looks like you, she said, not turning around, not knowing what else to say. She realized now that he was not sane in any known sense of the word, but she still hoped to talk her way out of it. She could feel the love seeping out of her. Her heart was dry ice.

It is me, he said sadly. *Don't be afraid.*

Where are we going? she said, because it was getting dark, and there was suddenly no floor.

Deeper, he said.

7.

Those ones. Why do women like them? They have nothing to offer, none of the usual things. They have short attention spans, falling-apart clothes, old beat-up cars, if any. The cars break down, and they try to fix them, and don't succeed, and give up. They go on long walks from which they forget to return. They prefer weeds to flowers. They tell trivial fibs. They perform clumsy tricks with oranges and pieces of string, hoping desperately that someone will laugh. They don't put food on the table. They don't make money. Don't, can't, won't.

They offer nothing. They offer the great clean sweep of nothing, the unseen sky during a blizzard, the dark pause between moon and moon. They offer their poverty, an empty wooden bowl; the bowl of a beggar, whose gift is to ask. Look into it, look down deep, where potential coils like smoke, and you might hear anything. Nothing has yet been said.

They have bodies, however. Their bodies are unlike the bodies of other men. Their bodies are verbalized. *Mouth, eye, hand, foot*, they say. Their bodies have weight, and move over the ground, step by step, like yours. Like you they roll in the hot mud of the sunlight, like you they are amazed by morning, like you they can taste the wind, like you they sing. *Love*, they say, and at the time they always mean it, as you do also. They can say *lust* as well, and *disgust*; you wouldn't trust them otherwise. They say the worst things you have ever dreamed. They open locked doors. All this is given to them for nothing.

They have their angers. They have their despair, which washes over them like gray ink, blanking them out, leaving them immobile, in metal kitchen chairs, beside closed windows, looking out at the brick walls of deserted factories, for years and years. Yet nothing is with them; it keeps faith with them, and from it they bring back messages:

Hurt, they say, and suddenly their bodies hurt again, like real bodies. *Death*, they say, making the word sound like the backwash of a wave. Their bodies die, and waver, and turn to mist. And yet they can exist in two worlds at once: lost in the earth or eaten by flames, and here. In this room, when you re-say them, in their own words.

But why do women like them? Not *like*, I mean to say: *adore*. (Remember that despite everything, despite all I have told you, the rusted cars, the greasy wardrobes, the lack of breakfasts, the hopelessness, remain the same.)

Because if they can say their own bodies, they could say yours also. Because they could say *skin* as if it meant something, not only to them but to you. Because one night, when the snow is falling and the moon is blotted out, they could put their empty hands, their hands filled with poverty, their beggar's hands, on your body, and bless it, and tell you it is made of light.

MY LIFE
AS A BAT

1. REINCARNATION

In my previous life I was a bat.

If you find previous lives amusing or unlikely, you are not a serious person. Consider: a great many people believe in them, and if sanity is a general consensus about the content of reality, who are you to disagree?

Consider also: previous lives have entered the world of commerce. Money can be made from them. *You were Cleopatra, you were a Flemish duke, you were a Druid priestess*, and money changes hands. If the stock market exists, so must previous lives.

In the previous-life market, there is not such a great demand for Peruvian ditch-diggers as there is for Cleopatra; or for Indian latrine-cleaners, or for 1952 housewives living in California split-levels. Similarly, not many of us choose to remember our lives as vultures, spiders, or rodents, but some of us do. The fortunate few. Conventional wisdom has it that reincarnation as an animal is a punishment for past sins, but perhaps it is a reward instead. At least a resting place. An interlude of grace.

Bats have a few things to put up with, but they do not inflict. When they kill, they kill without mercy, but without hate. They are immune from the curse of pity. They never gloat.

2.   NIGHTMARES

I have recurring nightmares.

In one of them, I am clinging to the ceiling of a summer cottage while a red-faced man in white shorts and a white V-necked T-shirt jumps up and down, hitting at me with a tennis racket. There are cedar rafters up here, and sticky flypapers attached with tacks, dangling like toxic seaweeds. I look down at the man's face, foreshortened and sweating, the eyes bulging and blue, the mouth emitting furious noise, rising up like a marine float, sinking again, rising as if on a swell of air.

The air itself is muggy, the sun is sinking; there will be a thunderstorm. A woman is shrieking, 'My hair! My hair!' and someone else is calling, 'Anthea! Bring the stepladder!' All I want is to get out through the hole in the screen, but that will take some concentration and it's hard in this din of voices, they interfere with my sonar. There is a smell of dirty bathmats – it's his breath, the breath that comes out from every pore, the breath of the monster. I will be lucky to get out of this alive.

In another nightmare I am winging my way – flittering, I suppose you'd call it – through the clean-washed demilight before dawn. This is a desert. The yuccas are in bloom, and I have been gorging myself on their juices and pollen. I'm heading to my home, to my home cave, where it will be cool during the burnout of day and there will be the sound of water trickling through limestone, coating the rock with a glistening hush, with the moistness of new mushrooms, and the other bats will chirp and rustle and doze until night unfurls again and makes the hot sky tender for us.

But when I reach the entrance to the cave, it is sealed over. It's blocked in. Who can have done this?

I vibrate my wings, sniffing blind as a dazzled moth over the hard surface. In a short time the sun will rise like a balloon on fire and I will be blasted with its glare, shriveled to a few small bones.

Whoever said that light was life and darkness nothing?

For some of us, the mythologies are different.

3.   VAMPIRE FILMS

I became aware of the nature of my previous life gradually, not only through dreams but through scraps of memory, through hints, through odd moments of recognition.

There was my preference for the subtleties of dawn and dusk, as opposed to the vulgar blaring hour of high noon. There was my déjà vu experience in the Carlsbad Caverns – surely I had been there before, long before, before they put in the pastel spotlights and the cute names for stalactites and the underground restaurant where you can combine claustrophobia and indigestion and then take the elevator to get back out.

There was also my dislike for headfuls of human hair, so like nets or the tendrils of poisonous jellyfish: I feared entanglements. No real bat would ever suck the blood of necks. The neck is too near the hair. Even the vampire bat will target a hairless extremity – by choice a toe, resembling as it does the teat of a cow.

Vampire films have always seemed ludicrous to me, for this reason but also for the idiocy of their bats – huge rubbery bats, with red Christmas-light eyes and fangs like a saber-toothed tiger's, flown in on strings, their puppet wings flapped sluggishly like those of an overweight and degenerate bird. I screamed at these filmic moments, but not with fear; rather with outraged laughter, at the insult to bats.

O Dracula, unlikely hero! O flying leukemia, in your cloak like a living umbrella, a membrane of black leather which you unwind from within yourself and lift like a stripteaser's fan as you bend with emaciated lust over the neck, flawless and bland, of whatever woman is longing for obliteration, here and now in her best negligee. Why was it given to you by whoever stole your soul to transform yourself into bat and wolf, and only those? Why not a vampire chipmunk, a duck, a gerbil? Why not a vampire turtle? Now that would be a plot.

4.   THE BAT AS DEADLY WEAPON

During the Second World War they did experiments with bats. Thousands of bats were to be released over German cities, at the hour of noon. Each was to have a small incendiary device strapped onto it, with a timer. The bats would have headed for darkness, as is their habit. They would have crawled into holes in walls, or secreted themselves under the eaves of houses, relieved to have found safety. At a preordained moment they would have exploded, and the cities would have gone up in flames.

That was the plan. Death by flaming bat. The bats too would have died, of course. Acceptable mega-deaths.

The cities went up in flames anyway, but not with the aid of bats. The atom bomb had been invented, and the fiery bat was no longer thought necessary.

If the bats had been used after all, would there have been a war memorial to them? It isn't likely.

If you ask a human being what makes his flesh creep more, a bat or a bomb, he will say the bat. It is difficult to experience loathing for something merely metal, however ominous. We save these sensations for those with skin and flesh: a skin, a flesh, unlike our own.

5.   BEAUTY

Perhaps it isn't my life as a bat that was the interlude. Perhaps it is this life. Perhaps I have been sent into human form as if on a dangerous mission, to save and redeem my own folk. When I have gained a small success, or died in the attempt – for failure, in such a task and against such odds, is more likely – I will be born again, back into that other form, that other world where I truly belong.

More and more, I think of this event with longing. The quickness of heartbeat, the vivid plunge into the nectars of crepuscular flowers, hovering in the infrared of night; the dank lazy half-sleep of daytime, with bodies rounded and soft as furred plums clustering around me, the mothers licking the tiny amazed faces of the newborn; the swift love of what will come next, the anticipations of the tongue and of the infurled, corrugated and scrolled nose, nose like a dead leaf, nose like a radiator grille, nose of a denizen of Pluto.

And in the evening, the supersonic hymn of praise to our Creator, the Creator of bats, who appears to us in the form of a bat and who gave us all things: water and the liquid stone of caves, the woody refuge of attics, petals and fruit and juicy insects, and the beauty of slippery wings and sharp white canines and shining eyes.

What do we pray for? We pray for food as all do, and for health and for the increase of our kind; and for deliverance from evil, which cannot be explained by us, which is hair-headed and walks in the night with a single white unseeing eye, and stinks of half-digested meat, and has two legs.

Goddess of caves and grottoes: bless your children.

HARDBALL

Here comes the future, rolling towards us like a meteorite, a satellite, a giant iron snowball, a two-ton truck in the wrong lane, careering downhill with broken brakes, and whose fault is it? No time to think about that. Blink and it's here.

How round, how firm, how fully packed is this future! How man-made! What wonders it contains, especially for those who can afford it! They are the elect, and by their fruits ye shall know them. Their fruits are strawberries and dwarf plums and grapes, things that can be grown beside the hydroponic vegetables and the toxin-absorbent ornamentals, in relatively little space. Space is at a premium, living space that is. All space that is not living space is considered dead.

Living space is under the stately pleasure dome, the work-and-leisure dome, the transparent bubbledome that keeps out the deadly cosmic rays and the rain sulfuric acid and the air which is no longer. No longer air, I mean. You can look out, of course: watch the sun, red at all times of day, rise across the raw rock and shifting sands, travel across the raw rock and shifting sands, set across the raw rock and shifting sands. The light effects are something.

But breathing is out of the question. That's a thing you have to do in here, and the richer you are, the better you do it. Penthouse costs a bundle; steerage is cramped, and believe me it stinks. Well, as they say, there's only so much to go around, and it wouldn't do if everyone got the same. No incentive then, to perform the necessary work, make the necessary sacrifices, inch your way up, to where the pale pink strawberries and the pale yellow carrots are believed, still, to grow.

What else is eaten? Well, there are no more hamburgers. Cows take up too much room. Chickens and rabbits are still cultivated, here and there; they breed quickly and they're small. Rats, of course, on the lower levels, if you can catch them. Think of the earth as an eighteenth-century ship, with stowaways but no destination.

And no fish, needless to say. None left in all that dirty water sloshing around in the oceans and through the remains of what used to be New York. If you're really loaded you can go diving there, for your vacation. Travel by airlock. Plunge into the romance of a bygone age. But it's an ill wind that blows nobody any good. No more street crime. Think of it as a plus.

Back to the topic of food, which will always be of interest. What will we have for dinner? Is it wall-to-wall bean sprouts? Apart from the pallid garnishes and the chicken-hearted hors d'oeuvres, what's the main protein?

Think of the earth as a nineteenth-century lifeboat, adrift in the open sea, with castaways but no rescuers. After a while you run out of food, you run out of water. You run out of everything but your fellow passengers.

Why be squeamish? Let's just say we've learned

the hard way about waste. Or let's say we all make our little contribution to the general welfare, in the end.

It's done by computer. For every birth there must be a death. Everything's ground up, naturally. Nothing you might recognize, such as fingers. Think of the earth as a hard stone ball, scraped clean of life. There are benefits: no more mosquitoes, no bird poop on your car. The bright side is a survival tool. So look on it.

I'm being unnecessarily brutal, you say. Too blunt, too graphic. You want things to go on the way they are, five square meals a day, new plastic toys, the wheels of the economy oiled and spinning, payday as usual, the smoke going up the chimney just the same. You don't like this future.

You don't like this future? Switch it off. Order another. Return to sender.

BREAD

Imagine a piece of bread. You don't have to imagine
it, it's right here in the kitchen, on the breadboard,
in its plastic bag, lying beside the bread knife. The
bread knife is an old one you picked up at an
auction; it has the word BREAD carved into the
wooden handle. You open the bag, pull back the
wrapper, cut yourself a slice. You put butter on it,
then peanut butter, then honey, and you fold it over.
Some of the honey runs out onto your fingers and
you lick it off. It takes you about a minute to eat the
bread. This bread happens to be brown, but there is

also white bread, in the refrigerator, and a heel of rye you got last week, round as a full stomach then, now going moldy. Occasionally you make bread. You think of it as something relaxing to do with your hands.

• • •

Imagine a famine. Now imagine a piece of bread. Both of these things are real but you happen to be in the same room with only one of them. Put yourself into a different room, that's what the mind is for. You are now lying on a thin mattress in a hot room. The walls are made of dried earth and your sister, who is younger than you are, is in the room with you. She is starving, her belly is bloated, flies land on her eyes; you brush them off with your hand. You have a cloth too, filthy but damp, and you press it to her lips and forehead. The piece of bread is the bread you've been saving, for days it seems. You are as hungry as she is, but not yet as weak. How long does this take? When will someone come with more bread? You think of going out to see if you might find something that could be eaten, but outside the streets are infested with scavengers and the stink of corpses is everywhere.

Should you share the bread or give the whole

piece to your sister? Should you eat the piece of bread yourself? After all, you have a better chance of living, you're stronger. How long does it take to decide?

• • •

Imagine a prison. There is something you know that you have not yet told. Those in control of the prison know that you know. So do those not in control. If you tell, thirty or forty or a hundred of your friends, your comrades, will be caught and will die. If you refuse to tell, tonight will be like last night. They always choose the night. You don't think about the night, however, but about the piece of bread they offered you. How long does it take? The piece of bread was brown and fresh and reminded you of sunlight falling across a wooden floor. It reminded you of a bowl, a yellow bowl that was once in your home. It held apples and pears; it stood on a table you can also remember. It's not the hunger or the pain that is killing you but the absence of the yellow bowl. If you could only hold the bowl in your hands, right here, you could withstand anything, you tell yourself. The bread they offered you is subversive, it's treacherous, it does not mean life.

• • •

There were once two sisters. One was rich and had no children, the other had five children and was a widow, so poor that she no longer had any food left. She went to her sister and asked her for a mouthful of bread. 'My children are dying,' she said. The rich sister said, 'I do not have enough for myself,' and drove her away from the door. Then the husband of the rich sister came home and wanted to cut himself a piece of bread; but when he made the first cut, out flowed red blood.

Everyone knew what that meant.

This is a traditional German fairy tale.

• • •

The loaf of bread I have conjured for you floats about a foot above your kitchen table. The table is normal, there are no trapdoors in it. A blue tea towel floats beneath the bread, and there are no strings attaching the cloth to the bread or the bread to the ceiling or the table to the cloth, you've proved it by passing your hand above and below. You didn't touch the bread though. What stopped you? You don't want to know whether the bread is real or whether it's just a hallucination I've somehow duped you into seeing. There's no doubt that you can see the bread, you can even smell it, it smells like yeast, and it looks solid enough, solid as your own arm. But can you trust it? Can you eat it? You don't want to know, imagine that.

POPPIES:

Three

Variations

In Flanders fields the poppies blow
Between the crosses, row on row.
That mark our place; and in the sky
The larks, still bravely singing, fly
Scarce heard amid the guns below.

— John McCrae

1.

I had an uncle once who served *in Flanders*. Flanders, or was it France? I'm old enough to have had the uncle but not old enough to remember. Wherever, those *fields* are green again, and plowed and harvested, though they keep throwing up rusty shells, broken skulls. *The* uncle wore a beret and marched in parades, though slowly. We always bought those felt *poppies*, which aren't even felt any more, but plastic: small red explosions pinned to your chest, like a *blow* to the heart. *Between the* other thoughts, that one *crosses* my mind. And the tiny lead soldiers in the shop windows, *row on row* of them, not lead any more, too poisonous, but every detail perfect, and from every part of the world: India, Africa, China, America. *That* goes to show, about war – in retrospect it becomes glamour, or else a game we think we could have played better. From time to time the stores *mark* them down, you can get bargains. There are some for us, too, with *our* new leafy flag, not the red rusted-blood one the men fought under. That uncle had *place*mats with the old flag, and cups *and* saucers. The planes *in the sky* were tiny then, almost comical, like kites with wind-up motors; I've seen them in movies. The uncle said he never saw *the larks*. Too much smoke, or fog. Too much roaring, though on some mornings it was very *still*. Those were the most dangerous. You hoped you would act *bravely* when the moment came, you kept up your courage by *singing*. There was a kind of *fly* that bred in the corpses, there were thousands of them he said; and during the bombardments you could *scarce* hear yourself think. Though sometimes you *heard* things anyway: the man beside him whispered, 'Look,' and when he looked there was no more torso: just a red hole, *a* wet splotch in *mid*air. That uncle's gone now too, the number of vets in the parade is smaller each year, they limp more. But in the windows *the* soldiers multiply, so clean and colorfully painted, with their little intricate *guns*, their shining boots, their faces, brown or pink or yellow, neither smiling nor frowning. It's strange to think how many soldiers like that have been owned over the years, loved over the years, lost over the years, in back yards or through gaps in porch floors. They're lying down there, under our feet in the garden and *below* the floorboards, armless or legless, faces worn half away, listening to everything we say, waiting to be dug up.

2.

Cup of coffee, the usual morning drug. He's off jogging, told her she shouldn't be so sluggish, but she can't get organized, it involves too many things:

the right shoes, the right outfit, and then worrying about how your bum looks, wobbling along the street. She couldn't do it alone anyway, she might get mugged. So instead she's sitting remembering how much she can no longer remember, of who she used to be, who she thought she would turn into when she grew up. *We are the dead*: that's about the only line left from *In Flanders Fields*, which she had to write out twenty times on *the* blackboard, for talking. When she was ten and thin, and now see. He says she should go vegetarian, like him, healthy as lettuce. She'd rather eat *poppies*, get the opiates straight from the source. Eat daffodils, the poisonous bulb like an onion. Or better, slice it into his soup. He'll *blow* his nose on her once too often, and then. *Between the* rock and the hard cheese, that's where she sits, inert as a prisoner, making little *crosses* on the wall, like knitting, counting the stitches *row on row, that* old trick to *mark* off the days. *Our place*, he calls this dump. He should speak for himself, she's just the mattress around here, she's just the cleaning lady, *and* when he ever lifts a finger there'll be sweet pie *in the sky*. She should burn *the* whole thing down, just for *larks; still*, however *bravely* she may talk, to herself, where would she go after that, what would she do?

She thinks of the bunch of young men they saw, downtown at night, where they'd gone to dinner, his birthday. High on something, *singing* out of tune, one guy's *fly* half open. Freedom. Catch a woman doing that, panty alert, she'd be jumped by every creep within a mile. Too late to make yourself *scarce*, once they get the skirt up. She's *heard* of a case like that, in a poolhall or somewhere. That's what keeps her in here, in this house, that's what keeps her tethered. It's not a *mid*life crisis, which is what he says. It's fear, pure and simple. Hard to rise above it. Rise above, like a balloon or *the* cream on milk, as if all it takes is hot air or fat. Or willpower. But the reason for that fear exists, it can't be wished away. What she'd need in real life is a few *guns*. That and the technique, how to use them. And the guts, of course. She pours herself another cup of coffee. That's her big fault: she might have the gun but she wouldn't pull the trigger. She'd never be able to hit a man *below* the belt.

3.

In school, when I first heard the word *Flanders* I thought it was what nightgowns were made of.

And pajamas. But then I found it was a war, more important to us than others perhaps because our grand-fathers were in it, maybe, or at least some sort of ancestor. The trenches, the *fields* of mud, the barbed wire, became our memories as well. But only for a time. Photographs fade, the rain eats away at statues, *the* neurons in our brains blink out one by one, and goodbye to vocabulary. We have other things to think about, we have lives to get on with. Today I planted five *poppies* in the front yard, orangey-pink, a new hybrid. They'll go well with the marguerites. Terrorists *blow* up airports, lovers slide blindly in *between the* sheets, in the soft green drizzle my cat *crosses* the street; in the spring regatta the young men *row on, row* on, as if nothing has happened since 1913, and the crowds wave and enjoy their tall drinks with cucumber and gin. What's wrong with *that?* We can scrape by, more or less, getting from year to year with hardly a *mark* on us, as long as we know *our place*, don't mouth off too much or cause uproars. A little sex, a little gardening, flush toilets and similar discreet pleasures; *and in the sky* the satellites go over, keeping a bright eye on us. The ospreys, *the* horned *larks*, the shrikes and the woodland warblers are having a thinner time of it, though *still bravely* trying to nest in the lacunae left by pesticides, the sharp blades of the reapers. If it's *singing* you want, there's lots of that, you can tune in any time; coming out of your airplane seatmate's earphones it sounds like a *fly* buzzing, it can drive you crazy. So can the news. Disaster sells beer, and this month hurricanes are the fashion, and famines: *scarce* this, scarce that, too little water, too much sun. With every meal you take huge bites of guilt. The excitement in the disembodied voices says: you *heard* it here first. Such *a* commotion in the *mid*-brain! Try meditation instead, be thankful for the annuals, for the smaller mercies. You listen, you listen to the moonlight, to the earthworms reveling in the lawn, you celebrate your own quick heartbeat. But below all that there's another sound, a groundswell, a drone, you can't get rid of it. It's the guns, which have never stopped, just moved around. It's the guns, still firing monotonously, bored with themselves but deadly, deadlier, deadliest, it's *the guns*, an undertone beneath each ordinary tender conversation. Say pass the sugar and you hear the guns. Say I love you. Put your ear against skin: below thought, below memory, *below* everything, the guns.

HOMELANDING

1.

Where should I begin? After all, you have never been there; or if you have, you may not have understood the significance of what you saw, or thought you saw. A window is a window, but there is looking out and looking in. The native you glimpsed, disappearing behind the curtain, or into the bushes, or down the manhole in the main street – my people are shy – may have been only your reflection in the glass. My country specializes in such illusions.

2.

Let me propose myself as typical. I walk upright on two legs, and have in addition two arms, with ten appendages, that is to say, five at the end of each. On the top of my head, but not on the front, there is an odd growth, like a species of seaweed. Some think this is a kind of fur, others consider it modified feathers, evolved perhaps from scales like those of lizards. It serves no functional purpose and is probably decorative.

My eyes are situated in my head, which also possesses two small holes for the entrance and exit of air, the invisible fluid we swim in, and one larger hole, equipped with bony protuberances called teeth, by means of which I destroy and assimilate certain parts of my surroundings and change them into my self. This is called eating. The things I eat include roots, berries, nuts, fruits, leaves, and the muscle tissues of various animals and fish. Sometimes I eat their brains and glands as well. I do not as a rule eat insects, grubs, eyeballs, or the snouts of pigs, though these are eaten with relish in other countries.

3.

Some of my people have a pointed but boneless external appendage, in the front, below the navel or midpoint. Others do not. Debate about whether the possession of such a thing is an advantage or a disadvantage is still going on. If this item is lacking, and in its place there is a pocket or inner cavern in which fresh members of our community are grown, it is considered impolite to mention it openly to strangers. I tell you this because it is the breach of etiquette most commonly made by tourists.

In some of our more private gatherings, the absence of cavern or prong is politely overlooked, like club feet or blindness. But sometimes a prong and a cavern will collaborate in a dance, or illusion, using mirrors and water, which is always absorbing for the performers but frequently grotesque for the observers. I notice that you have similar customs.

Whole conventions and a great deal of time have recently been devoted to discussions of this state of affairs. The prong people tell the cavern people that the latter are not people at all and are in reality more akin to dogs or potatoes, and the cavern people abuse the prong people for their obsession with images of poking, thrusting, probing, and stabbing. Any long object with a hole at the end, out of which various projectiles can be shot, delights them.

I myself – I am a cavern person – find it a relief not to have to worry about climbing over barbed wire fences or getting caught in zippers.

But that is enough about our bodily form.

4.

As for the country itself, let me begin with the sunsets, which are long and red, resonant, splendid and melancholy, symphonic you might almost say; as opposed to the short boring sunsets of other countries, no more interesting than a light switch. We pride ourselves on our sunsets. 'Come and see the sunset,' we say to one another. This causes everyone to rush outdoors or over to the window.

Our country is large in extent, small in population, which accounts for our fear of empty spaces, and also our need for them. Much of it is covered in water, which accounts for our interest in reflections, sudden vanishings, the dissolution of one thing into another. Much of it, however, is rock, which accounts for our belief in Fate.

In summer we lie about in the blazing sun, almost naked, covering our skins with fat and attempting to turn red. But when the sun is low in the sky and faint, even at noon, the water we are so fond of changes to something hard and white and cold and covers up the ground. Then we cocoon ourselves, become lethargic, and spend much of our time hiding in crevices. Our mouths shrink and we say little.

Before this happens, the leaves on many of our trees turn blood red or lurid yellow, much brighter and more exotic than the interminable green of jungles. We find this change beautiful. 'Come and see the leaves,' we say, and jump into our moving vehicles and drive up and down past the forests of sanguinary trees, pressing our eyes to the glass.

We are a nation of metamorphs.

Anything red compels us.

5.

Sometimes we lie still and do not move. If air is still going in and out of our breathing holes, this is called sleep. If not, it is called death. When a person has achieved death, a kind of picnic is held, with music, flowers, and food. The person so honored, if in one piece, and not, for instance, in shreds or falling apart, as they do if exploded or a long time drowned, is dressed in becoming clothes and lowered into a hole in the ground, or else burned up.

These customs are among the most difficult to explain to strangers. Some of our visitors, especially the young ones, have never heard of death and are bewildered. They think that death is simply one more of our illusions, our mirror tricks; they cannot understand why, with so much food and music, the people are sad.

But you will understand. You too must have death, among you. I can see it in your eyes.

6.

I can see it in your eyes. If it weren't for this I would have stopped trying long ago, to communicate with you in this halfway language which is so difficult for both of us, which exhausts the throat and fills the mouth with sand; if it weren't for this I would have gone away, gone back. It's this knowledge of death, which we share, where we overlap. Death is our common ground. Together, on it, we can walk forward.

By now you must have guessed: I come from another planet. But I will never say to you, take me to your leaders. Even I — unused to your ways though I am — would never make that mistake. We ourselves have such beings among us, made of cogs, pieces of paper, small disks of shiny metal, scraps of colored cloth. I do not need to encounter more of them.

Instead I will say, take me to your trees. Take me to your breakfasts, your sunsets, your bad dreams, your shoes, your nouns. Take me to your fingers; take me to your deaths.

These are worth it. These are what I have come for.

THE PAGE

1. The page waits, pretending to be blank. Is that its appeal, its blankness? What else is this smooth and white, this terrifyingly innocent? A snowfall, a glacier? It's a desert, totally arid, without life. But people venture into such places. Why? To see how much they can endure, how much dry light?

2. I've said the page is white, and it is: white as wedding dresses, rare whales, seagulls, angels, ice and death. Some say that like sunlight it contains all colors; others, that it's white because it's hot,

it will burn out your optic nerves; that those who stare at the page too long go blind.

3. The page itself has no dimensions and no directions. There's no up or down except what you yourself mark, there's no thickness and weight but those you put there, north and south do not exist unless you're certain of them. The page is without vistas and without sounds, without centers or edges. Because of this you can become lost in it forever. Have you never seen the look of gratitude, the look of joy, on the faces of those who have managed to return from the page? Despite their faintness, their loss of blood, they fall on their knees, they push their hands into the earth, they clasp the bodies of those they love, or, in a pinch, any bodies they can get, with an urgency unknown to those who have never experienced the full horror of a journey into the page.

4. If you decide to enter the page, take a knife and some matches, and something that will float. Take something you can hold onto, and a prism to split the light and a talisman that works, which

should be hung on a chain around your neck: that's for getting back. It doesn't matter what kind of shoes, but your hands should be bare. You should never go into the page with gloves on. Such decisions, needless to say, should not be made lightly.

There are those, of course, who enter the page without deciding, without meaning to. Some of these have charmed lives and no difficulty, but most never make it out at all. For them the page appears as a well, a lovely pool in which they catch sight of a face, their own but better. These unfortunates do not jump: rather they fall, and the page closes over their heads without a sound, without a seam, and is immediately as whole and empty, as glassy, as enticing as before.

5. The question about the page is: what is beneath it? It seems to have only two dimensions, you can pick it up and turn it over and the back is the same as the front. Nothing, you say, disappointed.

But you were looking in the wrong place, you were looking *on the back* instead of *beneath*. *Beneath the page* is another story. Beneath the page is a story. Beneath the page is everything that has ever happened, most of which you would rather not hear about.

The page is not a pool but a skin, a skin is there to hold in and it can feel you touching it. Did you really think it would just lie there and do nothing?

Touch the page at your peril: it is you who are blank and innocent, not the page. Nevertheless you want to know, nothing will stop you. You touch the page, it's as if you've drawn a knife across it, the page has been hurt now, a sinuous wound opens, a thin incision. Darkness wells through.

AN ANGEL

I know what the angel of suicide looks like. I have seen her several times. She's around.

She's nothing like the pictures of angels you run across here and there, the ones in classical paintings, with their curls and beautiful eyelashes, or the ones on Christmas cards, all cute or white. Much is made, in these pictures, of the feet, which are always bare, I suppose to show that angels do not need shoes: walkers on nails and live coals all of them, aspirin hearts, dandelion-seed heads, air bodies.

Not so the angel of suicide, who is dense, heavy

with antimatter, a dark star. But despite the differences, she does have something in common with those others. All angels are messengers, and so is she; which isn't to say that all messages are good. The angels vary according to what they have to say: the angel of blindness, for instance, the angel of lung cancer, the angel of seizures, the destroying angel. The latter is also a mushroom.

(Snow angels, you've seen them: the cold blank shape of yourself, the outline you once filled. They too are messengers, they come from the future. This is what you will be, they say, perhaps what you are: no more than the way light falls across a given space.)

Angels come in two kinds: the others, and those who fell. The angel of suicide is one of those who fell, down through the atmosphere to the earth's surface. Or did she jump? With her you have to ask.

Anyway, it was a long fall. From the friction of the air, her face melted off like the skin of a meteor. That is why the angel of suicide is so smooth. She has no face to speak of. She has the face of a gray egg. Noncommittal; though the shine of the fall still lingers.

They said, the pack of them, I will not serve. The angel of suicide is one of those: a rebellious waitress.

Rebellion, that's what she has to offer, to you, when you see her beckoning to you from outside the window, fifty stories up, or the edge of the bridge, or holding something out to you, some emblem of release, soft chemical, quick metal.

Wings, of course. You wouldn't believe a thing she said if it weren't for the wings.

THIRD

HANDED

The third hand is the one stamped in bear's grease and ocher, in charcoal and blood, on the walls of five-thousand-year-old caves; and in blue, on the doorposts, to ward off evil. It hangs in silver on a chain around the neck, signaling with its thumb; or, index finger extended, and with its golden wrist attached to an ebony stick, it strokes its way along the textural footpath, from Aleph to Omega. In churches it lurks in reliquaries, bony and bejeweled, or appears abruptly from fresco clouds, enormous and stern and significant, loud as a shout: Sin! Less elegant, banal even, and stenciled on a metal plate, it bosses us around: WAY OUT, it orders. UP HERE. WAY DOWN.

But these are merely pictures of it: roles, disguises, captured images, that in no way confine it. Do pictures of love confine love?

(The man and the woman walk down the street, hand in passionate hand; but whose hand is it really? It's the third hand each one holds, not the beloved's. It's the third hand that joins them together, the third hand that keeps them apart.)

The third hand is neither left nor right, dexter nor sinister. Consider the man who is caught in the act, red-handed, as they say. He proclaims his innocence, and why not believe him? *What ax?* he says. *I didn't know what I was doing, it wasn't me, and look, my hands are clean!* No one notices the third hand creeping away painfully on its fingers, like a stepped-on crab, trailing raw blood from its severed wrist.

But that happens only to those who have disowned it, who have cut it off and nailed it to a board and shut it up in a wall safe or a strongbox. It's light-fingered, the hand of a thief in the night; it will always get out, it will never hold still. It writes, and having written, moves. Moves on, dissolving, dissolving boundaries.

Vacant spaces belong to it, the vowel *o*, all blank pages, the number zero, the animals wolf and mole, the hour before birth and the minute after death, the loon, the owl, and all white flowers. The third hand opens doors, and closes them thoughtfully behind you. It is the other two that busy themselves with what goes on in the room.

The third hand is the hand the magician holds behind his back, while showing you the other two, candid and empty. *The hand is quicker than the eye*, he says. Notice that it's *hand*, singular. Only one. The third.

And when you walk through the snow, in the blizzard, growing cold and then unaccountably warmer, as night descends and sleep numbs you and you know you are lost, it's the third hand that slips confidingly into your own, a small hand, the hand of a child, leading you onward.

DEATH SCENES

I want to get the rosebushes in first. I like just sitting there. Last night there was a firefly. Can you imagine?

He said I could heal myself. He told me over the phone. He said, I can hear it in your voice. You should meditate on light for three minutes every day, and drink the leaves of cabbages, the leaves right next to the outer ones. Put them in a blender. Some garlic, too. You'll pee green but you'll heal. You know, it actually worked, for a while.

This is not attractive. I know it isn't, especially the

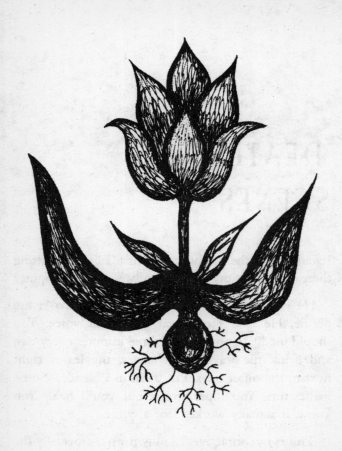

hair. What do I want? I want you to talk about normal things.

I know I look like hell. But it's still me in here. What do I want? I want you to talk about normal things. No I don't. I want you to look me in the eye and say, *I know you're dying*. But for Christ's sake don't make me console you.

I said, get the *fuck* out. This has nothing to do with my *fucking* attitude. Of course I'm bitter! Get out or I'll throw something at you. Where's the bedpan? You know I don't mean it. Christ I'd like a drink. Well, why not, eh?

No, don't. Don't hug me. It hurts.

I want to see what comes up, in the spring. Damn squirrels, they eat the bulbs. Mothballs are supposed to work.

If you want to cry, do it around the corner where she can't see you.

It's time for you to go home.

Something went wrong, we don't know what. We think you should come down at once.

— Can't you do something? It isn't her, it isn't her! She looks like the Pillsbury Doughboy, she's all swollen up, I can't stand it!

— It's not bothering her, she's in a coma.

— I don't believe in comas! She can hear, she can see everything! If you're going to talk about *death*, let's go down to the coffee shop.

It's cruel, it's cruel, she's never going to wake up! She can't get back into her body, and if she did she'd hate it! Can't somebody pull the plug?

I knew she'd died when the ashtray broke. It cracked right across. It was the one she gave me. I knew she was right there! It was her way of letting me know.

Glorious scenes. *Glorious* scenes! Nobody made scenes like hers. Vulgar as all get-out. Of course, she would always apologize afterwards. She needn't have done. Not to me.

What I miss is what she'd say. What she would have said. That's the difference: you have to put everything into the past conditional. *Bereft*, you might call it. Not her word, though – too po-faced. *That* was her word.

I went over there, did a little weeding. It's fading, though, what she looked like exactly. I can remember her tone of voice, but not her voice. It's funny the way you keep on talking to people. It's as if they could hear.

WE WANT
IT ALL

What we want of course is the same old story. The trees pushing out their leaves, fluttering them, shucking them off, the water thrashing around in the oceans, the tweedling of the birds, the unfurling of the slugs, the worms vacuuming dirt. The zinnias and their pungent slow explosions. We want it all to go on and go on again, the same thing each year, monotonous and amazing, just as if we were still behaving ourselves, living in tents, raising sheep, slitting their throats for God's benefit, refusing to invent plastics. For unbelief and bathrooms you pay a price.

If apples were the Devil's only bait we'd still be able to call our souls our own, but then the prick threw indoor plumbing into the bargain and we were doomed. Now we use up a lot of paper telling one another how to conserve paper, and the sea fills up with killer coffee cups, and we worry about the sun and its ambivalent rays.

When will it all cave in? The sky, I mean; our networks; our intricate pretensions. We were too good at what we did, at being fruitful, at multiplying, and now there's too much breathing. We eat dangerous foods, our shit glows in the dark, the cells of our bodies turn on us like sharks. Every system is self-limiting. Will we solve ourselves as the rats do? With war, with plagues, with mass starvation? These thoughts come with breakfast, like the juice from murdered fruits. Your depression, my friend, is the revenge of the oranges.

But we still find the world astounding, we can't get enough of it; even as it shrivels, even as its many lights flicker and are extinguished (the tigers, the leopard frogs, the plunging dolphin flukes), flicker and are extinguished, by us, by us, we gaze and gaze. Where do you draw the line, between love and greed? We never did know, we always wanted more. We want to take it all in, for one last time, we want to eat the world with our eyes.

Better than the mouth, my darling. Better than the mouth.

DANCE OF
THE
LEPERS

Who knows whether there could be such a thing? Possibly lepers do not dance, or are unable to. On the other hand, possibly they do. Somebody must know.

In the Dance of the Lepers, the lepers were not real. That is, they did not have leprosy. On the contrary. These lepers were healthy, able-bodied, and young. They were dancers. But they were pretending to be lepers, and since I always believe in surfaces, I believed that they were real.

The pretended, real dance of the lepers took place on a stage. It was Christmas up there. The music was quick, with nasal horns and light-fingered drums. People in medieval costumes whirled about. Muscular beggars were there, slender maidens in pointed caps with trailing veils, a stately prince, a voluptuous Gypsy, a witty fool. Everything you might require. Daydream ingredients. Takeout romance.

Then the lights dimmed and the music slowed, and the lepers entered. There were five of them; they held on to one another, to various parts of their various bodies, because they could not see. They were dressed in white strips of cloth wound round and round them, around their bodies and also around their hands and heads. They had no faces, only this blunt cloth.

They looked like animated mummies from an old horror film. They looked like living bedsheets. They looked like war casualties. They looked like cocoons. They looked like people you once knew very well, whose names you've forgotten. They looked like your own face in the steam-covered mirror after a bath, your own face temporarily nameless. They looked like aphasia. They looked like an ad for bandages. They looked like a bondage photo. They looked erotic. They looked obliterated. They looked like a sad early death.

The music they danced to was filled with the ringing of bells. In fact they carried little bells, little iron bells, or so I seem to remember. That was to warn people: stay away from the lepers. Or: stay away from the dance. Dancing can be dangerous.

What about their dance? There is very little I can tell you about that. One thing is certain: it was not a tap dance. Also: no pirouettes.

It was a dance of supplication, a numb dance, a dance of hopelessness and resignation. Also: a dance of continuation, a dance of going on despite everything, a stubborn dance. An awkward, hampered dance. A fluid, graceful dance. A clumsy, left-footed, infinitely skillful dance. A cynical and disgusted dance, a dance of worship, naive and joyful. A dance.

Ah lepers. If you can dance, even you, why not the rest of us?

GOOD
BONES

1.

You have good bones, they used to say, and I paid no attention. What did I care about good bones, then? I was more concerned with what was covering them. I was more concerned with lust, and pimples. The bones were backdrop.

Now they are growing into their own, those bones. Flesh diminishes, giving way to bedrock. Structural principles. What you need is the right light, to blot out the wrinkles, the incidentals. The right shade, the right amount of sun, and see, out come the bones, the good bones, the bones come out like flowers.

2.

Them bones, them bones, them dry bones, them and their good connections; we sang them over once around the campfire, those gleeful strutters to the Word of the Lord, or to our own hands clapping. Behind each face, each lovely body in its plaid shirt, soft bum on hard granite, I could guess the Halloween skeleton, white and one-dimensional, a chalk bone-head drawn on a blackboard; a zombie, a brief *memento mori*, dragged out for burning, like a heretic, flanked by the torches of the incandescent marshmallows.

Our voices made short work of them, them bones. Tossed on the bonfire they flared up like butter, and went out and were dismissed. *You are my sunshine*, we sang, though not to them. We nestled closer, jellify-ing each other, some of us boneless.

So much for death. So much for death, at that time, there.

3.

This is the cemetery. The good bones are in here, the bad bones are out there, beyond the church wall, beyond the pale, unsanctified.

The bad bones behaved badly, perhaps because of bad blood, bad luck, bad childhoods. Anyway, they did not treat their bodies well. Walked them over cliff edges, jumped them off bell towers. Tried to fly. Broke things.

The good bones lie snug under their tidy monuments. They have been given brooches to wear, signet rings, poems carved on stone, marble urns, citations. Circlets of bright hair. They have been worthy and dutiful, they deserve it. That's what it says here: the last word.

The bad bones have been bad, so they are better left unsaid. They are better left unsaying. But they were never happy, they always wanted more, they were always hungry. They can smell the words, the words coming out of your mouth all warm and yeasty. They want some words of their own. They'll be back.

4.

This is my friend, these are her bones, these ashes we pour out under the tulips. When she fell down on the sidewalk her hipbone shattered. It was hollow in there, eaten away, like a tree with ants. Bone meal.

They put her in the hospital and I went to see her. I'm terrified, she said, but it's sort of interesting. My turds are white, like bird turds. It's calcium. I'm dissolving myself, I'm shitting bones. I guess you can do worse than be fertilizer. Other things can grow.

We are both fond of gardens.

5.

Today I speak to my bones as I would speak to a dog.
I want to go up the stairs, I tell them. Up, up, up,
with one leg dragging. Is the ache deep in the bones,
this elusive pain? Does that mean it will rain? Good
bones, *good* bones, I coax, wondering how to reward
them; if they will sit up for me, beg, roll over, do
one more trick, once more.

There. We're at the top. *Good* bones! Good *bones!*
Keep on going.

Also by Margaret Atwood

MORNING IN THE BURNED HOUSE

'Margaret Atwood is the quiet Mata Hari, the mysterious, violent figure . . . who pits herself against the ordered, too-clean world like an arsonist'

— *Michael Ondaatje*

Margaret Atwood's first new book of poems for over a decade is cause for celebration. By turns dark, playful and intimate – these poems are Atwood's most mature, 'setting foot on the middle ground / between body and word'. Here is that wickedly dry, humorous voice – and here too are personal poems that concern themselves with love, with memory, with the fragility of the natural world.

THE ROBBER BRIDE

'It stirs depths that *Cat's Eye* did not reach, and grants deeper, stronger powers to women's friendship in distress'

— *Marina Warner*

Zenia is beautiful, smart and greedy, by turns manipulative and vulnerable, needy and ruthless. She is also dead. Just to make absolutely sure Tony, Roz and Charis are there for the funeral. But five years on, as the three women share a decorous lunch, the unthinkable happens: 'with waves of ill will flowing out of her like cosmic radiation,' Zenia is back . . .

THE HANDMAID'S TALE

'Superlative'
— *Angela Carter*

'Moving, vivid and terrifying. I only hope it is not prophetic'
— *Conor Cruise O'Brien*

The Republic of Gilead allows Offred only one function: to breed. If she deviates, she will, like all dissenters, be hanged at the wall or sent out to die slowly of radiation sickness. But even a repressive state cannot obliterate desire — neither Offred's nor that of the two men on whom her future hangs.

LADY ORACLE

'If you feel safe only with "nine to five" reality, you'll probably not enjoy her books. But if you'd like to lift-off, try her'

— *Cosmopolitan*

'A really gifted writer . . . a mistress of controlled hysteria'

— *Time*

From fat girl to thin, from red hair to mud brown, from Polish count to radical husband, from writer of romances to distinguished poet — Joan Foster is utterly confused by her life of multiple identities. She decides to escape to an Italian seaside resort to take stock of her life. But first, she must plan her death . . .

LIFE BEFORE MAN

'A splendid work . . . It is superb, complete'
> — *Marilyn French*

'A modern saga . . . she has a fine ear for words and a quick wit for absurdities'
> — *The Times*

Elizabeth, monstrous yet pitiable; Nate, her husband, a patchwork man, gentle, disillusioned; Lesje, a young woman at the natural history museum, for whom dinosaurs are as important as men. A sexual triangle; three people in thrall to the tragicomedy we call love.

SURFACING

'One of the most important novels of the twentieth century . . . utterly remarkable'
— *New York Times*

'A novelist and poet of great gifts'
— *Guardian*

'A stunning and satisfying book'
— *Time Out*

A young divorcee returns to the remote island of her childhood in Northern Canada to investigate the mysterious disappearance of her father. Flooded with memories, she is gradually drawn back into her past as the wild island exerts its elemental hold . . .

WILDERNESS TIPS

A leathery bog-man transforms an old love affair; a
sweet, gruesome gift is sent to the wife of an ex-
lover; landscape paintings are haunted by the ghost
of a young girl. This dazzling collection of short
stories takes us into familiar Atwood territory to
reveal the many textures of contemporary life and
the logic of irrational behaviour.